CHOKE
BOX

CHOKE BOX

a Fem-Noir

CHRISTINA MILLETTI

UNIVERSITY OF MASSACHUSETTS PRESS
Amherst and Boston

ISBN 978-1-62534-425-0 (paper)

Designed by Jen Jackowitz
Set in Crimson Text and ITC Officina
Printed and bound by Maple Press, Inc.

Cover design by CPorter Designs, llc
Cover illustration by Anst F. Reichhold, lithograph in Dr. Otto Zuckerkandl's *Atlas and Epitome of Operative Surgery* (1902). https://catalog.hathitrust.org/Record/001586476.

Library of Congress Cataloging-in-Publication Data

Names: Milletti, Christina, author.
Title: Choke box : a fem-noir / Christina Milletti.
Description: Amherst : University of Massachusetts Press, [2019] |
    Identifiers: LCCN 2018051828 (print) | LCCN 2018055291 (ebook) | ISBN
    9781613766743 () | ISBN 9781613766750 () | ISBN 9781625344250 | ISBN
    9781625344250 (paperback)
Classification: LCC PS3613.I56266 (ebook) | LCC PS3613.I56266 C48 2019
    (print) | DDC 813/.6—dc23
LC record available at https://lccn.loc.gov/2018051828

British Library Cataloguing-in-Publication Data
A catalog record for this book is available from the British Library.

This book is not a work of fiction.

No names or identifying details have been changed to protect the innocent. There are no innocents in this book, not even the rosy-cheeked infant who makes brief but regular cameos. Like all babies, she sucked her mother dry and spat her out. Isn't that the way of the world?

Any resemblance to real persons, living or dead, is wholly intended by the author who has re-created in the following pages all the situations, locales, conversations, and dreams that she committed to memory long before her civil commitment. In truth, there's nothing else for her to do but to re-create the past from memory now—fortunately, her therapist and her attorney encourage her work—so any disputes should be referred back to the doubter, not the author, who has at every turn dedicated herself to the truth, the whole truth, and nothing but the truth. Simply put? She has nothing to hide and as her tween son likes to say: she's much too slow to pull a fast one.

The fact is she can't lie through her teeth, like a rug, or a tombstone. She's never pulled the wool over anyone's eyes. As for cock and bull stories? See her husband. If you can find him.

There are so many ways in which there is no crime.
—*Gertrude Stein*

For all the madwomen in their attics.
You know who you are.

CHOKE
BOX

CHAPTER ONE

The So-Called Butter Knife Affair

The assault that took place two years ago on the reasonably bright morning of April 11 wasn't the incident that led to my incarceration. The "So-Called Butter Knife Affair" (as the nurses here call it) wasn't responsible for my family's downward spiral as court documents allege. Yet the Board at Buffalo Psychiatric highlights the episode at every hearing. On every file. For them, that day with my son is the pivotal moment in the (incomplete) history I've compiled here, the lynchpin whose sudden collapse led to my family's swift and complete devolution. I've tried to explain to the Board that they're far off the mark. I've pointed out other forces, factual and spectral, at work. But the truth blunts my tongue. My words are rough and fur-coated.

Somewhere, my husband writes:

The truth does not—will not—set you free.

I try to be forgiving.

I remind myself I'd have to be sylvan-tongued, svelte (and at least ten years younger) to convince the men and women who now own my life—the tired nurses in their cheerful, bleached scrubs; the Board of myopic doctors who mind them—that my assault of a ten-year-old boy over blueberry pancakes took place as they say.

Just not the way they think.

Since it's my son's interests they have at heart, I brace myself each time they read excerpts from the police report to me: a boy and his mother alone in a kitchen. The boy sitting down at the table whole. Then rising from it bloody and damp not ten minutes later, a butter knife buried up to its hilt in the lean muscles of his taut hairless thigh. The puddle of blood at his feet, deep enough and thick enough that, when a housecat later dipped her paws in it, the blood filled in the prints at once, congealing where she bent over the lip of the pool to sample her young master's pap.

It's all there in the record, the Board reminds me.

What they never acknowledge? I told the officer working the case—a Lieutenant Jaffe, if memory serves—those details myself. You'd think that would be enough to convince them I've nothing to hide. Instead, they focus on what they call "related fine points" like an aging bustle of slow-moving aunts fretting over the frayed edges of a bent doily.

"Where," Board Member 3 asks, as though he's never asked the question before, "did the butter knife come from?"

"And why," BM1 chimes in, "did you cancel your doctor appointment," (he hesitates, flips through my file), "a *standing* chiropractic appointment just minutes before the 'incident'" (he deploys the word dryly) "happened?"

BM6 doesn't wait for an answer. His voice is as yellowed and faded as the pages of an old book. Both my counselor and I must lean in to hear him.

"Please characterize," he says, not even trying to project his thin, reedy voice, "your husband's relationship with Regina Hammond."

To this BM3 adds at once: "And describe your mood since your daughter was born."

Naturally, I have answers to all their questions. The Board has heard them before. Now they will hear them again: the repetitions, not the replies themselves, are the focus of our Wednesday morning meetings. Perhaps I'll change my story (they think). Perhaps, then, they'll catch me out.

But how do you "catch out" the truth?

Fortunately, my counselor Celeste has trained me well. "Well-paced precision," she instructs, is the chief trait I must exhibit. "It's a sign of respect as well as sanity."

She gives me a long look. "Do your best."

Celeste has always been direct with me. So I keep it together. For her.

I sit up straight, I fold my hands. I try to keep the quiver from my voice.

I answer the Board's questions calmly. Deliberately. While, inside, I swear at Ed. You swine-deviled spunk of a man, I think. Just look at what you've done.

Answer 1: I bought the knife, with cash, from a local retailer (the receipt, of course, is now long gone). Our neighbors, the Hammonds, were due at the time to come over for dinner—a fact, I reminded them, that neither Regina nor her (now) ex-husband, Bernard, dispute.

Answer 2: Because I was tired. So very tired. More tired than they could imagine. As they knew, my daughter was (then) nine months old. What they didn't know? She was a lousy sleeper: I hadn't slept for more than two consecutive hours since the strange night of her birth. So it wasn't unusual for me to cancel hair, dentist, even chiropractic appointments (a fact they could check). If she finally broke down and slept, I'd nap myself. Isn't that what every parenting guide advises?

The answer to their third question was trickier. As Celeste knew, I'd discovered that Ed was sleeping with Regina Hammond. But to admit what I knew (as BM6 implied) gave the Board what they wanted: a motive. So Celeste had advised me not to lie, but to keep my tone what she called—with her charming, mild-mannered acidity—"light."

I did my best.

I imagined my anger taking a buoyant form: perhaps a hot-air balloon lifting my husband skyward. Directly into a bank of wires.

"Ed was flirtatious," I said (again). "A charmer. And my neighbor, as I'm sure you've noticed, endures compliments with admirable skill."

The way a flytrap endures flies.

Their last question about my mood? That was a real problem. A case of postpartum depression would explain everything as far as they were concerned—make sense of a senseless act—and if I'd just admit to a bad case of "baby blues," the Board could go home, take their kids to a park, and feel as though their world were in order. Bobby's wound, my convincing grief, even my history as a so-called "good citizen": my entire case would fall into place and the Board wouldn't look any further. Of course the vast majority of PPD sufferers who end up "acting out" (as the Board says politely) tend to kill their children, not the men in their lives, as I've since learned. But it would explain the fly in my file's ointment—the memory lapse that continues to plague me—and why, "even now," as they see it, I remain unable to recognize my (then) so-called "altered" state of mind myself.

Hell, it's persuasive logic even to me.

On the bad days, I comfort myself that I could not face such an allegation if the Board's suspicion—that I deliberately hurt Bobby—had any merit. That only a sane woman pushed to the point of despair would consider any diagnosis bantered about by six sodden-faced men with intolerable ease. But I must. I've been in the room with death before. It smells like piss and stale sheets. Florid breath over a rotten tooth. The fine particulate of the body's corruption remains trapped like sand in your nose hairs.

I never want to smell it again.

The Board should know that. They know my history after all: about my brother, Jules (his conspicuous death). And from Jules's best-selling books, all about my mother Helena (her persistent life). My job is to convince them I'm not broken: that my childhood didn't wind me up and send me spinning into a dervishly murderous future.

I don't blame their fear. The precedents of women who act out are frightening. Women who give up. Who give in. Mothers whose minds unravel when their children's worlds replace their own. Women who kill when they realize— suddenly—that they never existed as the sleek, unfettered anatomical engines they still remember, because they never did for the sweet tots for whom they selflessly care.

We are nothing more than memory. So it's the simplest, most complete annihilation to be forgotten by those we love—particularly when the amnesiacs are seedling reflections of yourself.

And their father has forgotten too.

Suddenly, a whispered question from Ed:

How much worse, Jane, could death be?

In an ancient religion from the Greek Peloponnese (I've learned during my regularly scheduled "Library Encounter Times" or "L.E.T.'s," as inmates like me ironically call them because they "let" us have so little here), the most promising initiates were given the option of drinking water from one of two rivers: Mnemosyne or Lethe. The former offered omniscience, the latter, amnesia. Both choices led to death after an intense (all too brief) period of oracular insight.

Memory is killing—that's the truth—and mothers know as much intuitively. Infanticides might take the low road. The rest of us, the more circuitous high road. But all mothers travel with the same baggage—the corpse of the woman we once were. Some of us can no longer remember her fully. Others can't put her from our minds. But it's memory, in the end, that drives mothers to madness—to kill their children— which is not unlike saying, to kill themselves.

Which leads me to wonder: is it psychosis, or the height of logic, to do away with a body that's been done *in*? Is murder an unnatural act if you believe you're already dead?

Of course I'm wicked for thinking such thoughts. Celeste knows I know it (she's heard such turns in logic from me before) and, as usual, she takes it all in stride with her simple smile, advising me only to "keep my own counsel" when we meet with the Board.

"Better yet, save it all for the book." There is a soft touch on my arm.

She always gives sound advice.

I'm not so foolish as to think the Board is capable of assessing my more internecine thoughts with subtlety or nuance. Their world is simple by need: a woman who troubles to understand a murderer's motives has likely committed murder herself. A "mimetic socio-pathology," my court-appointed therapist calls it. Yet I'd argue (if they'd ever give me the chance) that it is precisely my capacity for imagining the mindset of a murderess that, paradoxically, makes my claim— that I'm not one myself—far more convincing. That it's my ability to envision the worst that prevents me from strolling idly down dark, fevered paths.

After all, what else is murder, but a failure of imagination?

The one lesson I've learned in the past several months is that we cannot fear the dark places to which the mind turns in the twilight hours. Like a cat, we must look long and deep: we must see as clearly at midnight as we do at noon. Who wouldn't shudder at the shadows we cast. The silhouette of hands around a neck. A rigid back hunched over a bathtub's still waters. But we have to come to terms with what we glimpse in our most hidden corners.

It is dangerous to look.

But it's even more wicked to look away.

I will try to describe in the pages that follow what I've seen in my kitchen and bedroom and my mind's secret corners. I will tell the whole truth, nothing but the truth—though not because I wish to (haven't I said I'll be frank?) or because (as the Board will surely propose) I exhibit all the telltale signs of a closet exhibitionist. Not even because I have prior experience ghostwriting memoirs and I've come to use the candid voice I adopt for my work to describe my private world as well. For the first time in my life I can thank my brother Jules for that.

Let me directly address the Board's implied diagnosis—their preferred line of interrogation—so that it doesn't lurk beneath the pages that follow:

It was with sound mind and body that I hurt my son, Robert Edward Tamlin, one bright April morning.

It was my knife. I was holding it.

Bobby's injury occurred while he sat less than four feet from me.

What I dispute—and what I will go on to dispute to the end of my days—is that I am "at fault" for his wound. Let me pose this assertion another way: while "I" threw the knife, I am not to blame for throwing it.

The "I" whom the Board describes in their files?

The "I" about whom Ed, even now, still writes?

Like a toad in a slowly boiling pot of water, that "I" has been subject to malicious forces beyond her control.

Wherever he is, I can hear Ed as clearly as if he's standing beside me:

Come on, Jane. Really?

One more time. For the record, goddammit.

I am not to blame.

CHAPTER TWO

Mnemosyne or Lethe

The truth?

I'll never know—precisely—how Bobby was injured that morning. I distinctly remember where I was standing in our spare, sunlit kitchen. I even recall what I was doing before the knife flew. But how one thing *led* to the other—what my therapist calls "cycle cognition"—has disappeared from my mind completely. First it was there. And then it was not. And where it has gone no one can tell.

I have no memory at all of that moment. Six seconds forever lost to me now.

I do know it was a school day. Upstairs, Ed was already hard at work on his book—his "memoir," he called it. Since he'd started writing, he'd taken to sleeping on the couch in his study in order to, he claimed, "expedite his memory." And it was left to me to wake up our son, push him into the bathroom, then persuade him to brush his teeth, wash his face, and wrestle his cowlick into place—all the while bracing the baby with my tender left tennis elbow. Then, down to the kitchen the three of us went for breakfast, only twenty minutes before the school bus arrived to take Bobby to Harris Hill Elementary. With the exception of Ed's growing remoteness (not so very different from that of other fathers who leave for work before their children wake), our family that morning could have been any other in our neighborhood. The sun streamed through the windows. The smell of lawn pesticides lingered above the dew in the air. The baby drooled on a toy in her playpen. It was peaceful. Boring even. I'm sure I felt restless.

Now I miss those days the way an amputee misses a limb.

As usual, Bobby was running late, his book bag was only half packed, and he was wearing two different socks. But he was in a good mood and, as the socks could fool for a match, I let him go on yammering about a presentation he had to give that afternoon in science class about the "seasonal migrations of polar bears." He was acting cocky. Evidently, his friend/nemesis (I couldn't keep track) Jimmy Hammond had begged their teacher, Ms. Stuttgart—a stout woman with three cats and no children—for the same assignment. But perhaps because Jimmy often gave her a tough time at recess, she'd given him a report on chicken farming instead. The upshot: chickens weren't cool, Jimmy wasn't happy, and Bobby had become the current target of his friend's unfocused tween fury.

"He's p.o.'d," Bobby grinned.

It was one of Ed's pet phrases, one I'd always disliked. It made Ed sound peevish, like an old lady fussing over a pile of dog crap on her front lawn. Maybe that's why, when Bobby said it that day, he made me smile—a boy channeling a father impersonating a crabby octogenarian. Bobby's squeaky adolescent pitch was corrective: in it, I could hear Ed's voice. But because it was Bobby, not Ed, I laughed.

"Really?" I said.

Bobby nodded, diving into his pancake. "He lied and told Josh I liked his girlfriend, that he caught me . . . ," he paused and I knew he was censoring a pill of saucy language that no doubt involved his nether regions. "In any case," he quickly went on, "he said some stupid stuff on the bus yesterday."

"Really." This time my tone had flatlined. But he didn't notice.

"So I said Jimmy's got skid marks in his underwear. That his socks are yellow." He coughed, choked on his breakfast. "It's true. They're *gross*."

I'm sure I rolled my eyes. I'm sure I meant to lecture him on the long-term rewards of generosity and self-respect. Would have advised tolerance for the body's inevitable corruption. Had events played out differently, Bobby no doubt would have listened and, with his mild earnestness, tamped down the fit that was cracking him up. At least, he would have put the hand clutching his denimed crotch back on the table where it belonged.

But as syrup dripped from his chin, and he smacked his lips contentedly, I held my tongue, saved the lecture for another day. I was tired and there was nothing to worry about. Bobby could fend for himself. And I had to let him grow up, grow out and away from me. *Become his own man*, as Ed liked to say. Soon I'd just be his appendage, his cook. The weekend driver. Needed but not necessary. In no time at all, my son would have real secrets. Soon there would be dates. Locked bedroom doors. Pheromones. Sweat. Abused athletic socks. Right now, I reminded myself, his heart was light. My son was sweet. Bobby was as impressionable as clay.

"Talk to your father," I advised, then flipped a pancake. A moment later, I slid it onto his plate.

It is a feature of motherhood that, even after all the accusations that have been leveled my way this past year, I feel most guilty for this simple, offhand remark. I knew Ed wouldn't answer a knock on his door and, though Bobby was long-limbed and fast, Jimmy Hammond—a sweaty, bloated-faced boy who smelled like old onions—always enjoyed roughing kids up. Bully was in his future. Everyone knew it.

Everyone but his mother, Regina.

A birdlike woman who wore her shoulders like wings, Regina often chirped at parties about her son's wit, while Jimmy's wiry, absentminded father looked on in disbelief. If she hadn't cut such a great figure, as my mother used to say, she would have been insufferable. Instead, I fantasized about her waist size (the entire neighborhood fantasized about her in one way or another) and wondered, once again, about the origin of Jimmy's enigmatic pedigree. It's not too much to say that I wasn't the only woman who hoped that if I just stayed in her orbit, offered unrepentant approval, Regina's charisma would rub off on me. Maybe I'd even get a little of what she was getting from the sturdy, studded pool boy who stopped by her home on Thursday mornings while Bernard was off at work.

We all have fantasies, right?

As for Ed? He rolled his eyes at the neighborhood gossip.

"It's nice to see a woman get what she wants," I said, backing myself against his crotch, knocking him mildly off balance. He laughed, cuffed me away.

"Maybe later," he said.

As usual, later never came.

Now I wonder: was that the instant Regina appeared on his radar? Would this story have been completely different if I'd just kept my thoughts, my soft-boiled ass, to myself?

How naïve. My bile rises up, burns the back of my tongue. It's not the first time. I choke.

Of course, I wouldn't have had to look so hard for the piranha hiding within the school of sharks if Ed hadn't moved us east of Buffalo to the suburb of Clarence, to a so-called "gateway development zone"—an experimental neighborhood built by one of his clients, wedged between the muscular outer suburbs and the posh inner exurbs designed to appeal (so the pamphlet read) to "young, upwardly mobile homeowners looking for outer space and inner peace, for self-discovery and future fortune. Mean Age: 38. No. of Children: 1. No. of Cars: 2. No. of Homes: 1.5."

Ed's client had built the community on the homestead of an old barley estate. The original farmhouse itself was in good condition, and it stood at the center of an enormous cul de sac where the development brochure still pictures (I'm told) a "community center anchored by an organic garden, kite shop, gallery space, and day spa." Ed whistled when he showed it to me. The new homes were a marvel, tricked out with solar panels, geothermal floors, whirlpools, saunas, and media rooms. "Our house will be at the center of all that," he said. "Not bad for an old barley farm, right?"

True, the old farmhouse was a steal. Ed was doing his wealthy client a favor. All that fresh air, meanwhile, was terrific for Bobby. But couldn't we have foreseen the effect our new old home would have on us? Shouldn't we have known that moving into a farmhouse—no matter how quaintly maintained or historically fetching—surrounded by a dozen newly pointed mini-mansions was simply a bad idea? That our neighbors, high on the chemical outgas of new home aroma, would begin to resent the mortality our farmhouse cast right in their sightline? All too soon, we'd feel under siege, all those eyes on us, just waiting for the house to be razed.

It was supposed to be a temporary arrangement. "Just one year," Ed assured me. After that, his client was going to pay us a reasonable markup to move out, knock the farmhouse over, and build the spa in its place. The plans were on course. And then the Clarence Center Historical Society got wind of the scheme. Suddenly, the farmhouse was the county's "last emblem of pre-Fordian Agriculture & Animal Matrimonial Heritage." A legal intervention was filed and we weren't stuck so much as waylaid in lawsuits against both Ed's client and Erie County. One year became two. And when Ed wouldn't settle, his law firm, wearied of what his colleagues called his "lack of focus," asked him to take a leave of absence. Embarrassed, annoyed, my stubborn husband did just that. Then started writing. Not long after, he officially quit his job. And once our credit tanked, Ed's tune about the farmhouse changed. I wasn't surprised. His new pitch was even persuasive. "We're the cheapest house in an upscale neighborhood," he argued. "Moving?" He waved his hands about. "Why would we want to do that? When we settle or sell—when my book is done— we'll make a killing. Move wherever we want."

"We'll show them," he said, pointing outside vaguely. At the time, I thought he meant our neighbors. The Historical Society staff. The firm. His former client. My mother.

Ed said it more firmly the second time: "We'll show them what's *what*."

I must have sighed, because he wrapped me up in his arms. "Come on, Janey." He was so warm then. "Let's just see it through."

Ed wasn't just a lawyer. He was a salesman too. I suppose all lawyers are.

So I held my tongue. But our neighbors' front lawns were our front lines, and all that staring wore me down. Pre-dawn joggers and post-breakfast strollers. Loose children and lost dogs. Midnight insomniacs and early risers. It wasn't the looking itself that troubled me. Even I look into other people's windows. Often, I'll admit, intentionally. But our family had made a subtle move from curiosity to *entertainment*. We were "them." The hothouse drama at center stage. We didn't belong. And it became more than evident as our neighbors sat on their porches sipping cocktails and nibbling overpriced cheese that they excused their bad behavior because they believed we were conditional. "Visitors" at best. "Interlopers" at worst. We'd be gone soon enough. So they lurked and peeped, scrutinized our dull programming of getting to work, reprimanding our children, washing dishes, plunging toilets, picking noses, paying bills. How humdrum, I thought. Still they watched. Their hot eyes fixed on the backs of our necks.

I can't fully blame the farmhouse for our troubles, though. It didn't make us the family we became. The house just set us into relief, made our hidden problems stand out, the way you can only distinguish a deep shade of navy from black by setting the two colors side by side in the direct light of the sun.

Of all our neighbors, Regina Hammond seemed the most sincere. Which is to say, she craved sincerity the way a goldfish craves ocean, an idea out of her depth.

I try to be kind to myself: how could I have known she had her eye on Ed? That she'd suck off my husband while I nursed in the next room? That by the time I'd fixed my shirt, he'd fixed his fly. A wild symmetry of domestic proportions.

The moral of the story is simple: the nicest neighbors behind your fence can be malevolent once they walk through your gate.

Don't let their feet crush your grass. Or stir up the brush.

Duck your head. Turn the hasp.

And don't let them see your fear.

On that April morning, I was focused on getting Bobby to the bus on time with a hot meal in his stomach. My movements were economical from long experience. I signed a test, flipped a pancake, made myself a cup of coffee without moving more than two feet in any direction. I even spared a moment to coo to the baby who, sitting hunched like a frog in her playpen, was happily beating a wood spoon on the rail, making the kind of insistent, percussive music only infant ears can love.

For a mother, I was at peak performance.

How little I once knew.

Bobby kept talking. I washed the dishes. Our cat, Charlie Parker, had curled up at my feet. I had hold of a plate, a pan, a carton of milk. I barely listened as Bobby rambled on about his report—on polar bears, ice floes, and mortality rates—when I began to wash the butter knife. Why it was out, I'll never know. At the time, I'm sure I thought Ed had merely taken it out of the drawer by mistake before he went up to his office to work. He knew as much about butter knives as he did about salad forks: it was all the same to him.

I soaped the butter knife. There was a small stain on the handle that would not come off. So as anyone might, I soaped the knife, rinsed it again. Raising it high in the sunlight, I turned it about to get a good look. The light glinted. I saw my face in the blade.

At that same moment in his study upstairs, I now know Ed must have typed in his memoir:

Then the knife wasn't in her hands.

Because, suddenly, the knife *wasn't* in my hands.

And Charlie Parker began to hiss.

What happened at that moment isn't so much a blur as a series of disconnected snapshots: six seconds unmoored in my mind, awash in a sea of disbelief. How could the knife have slipped from my hand with such surprising force? Such fortuitous aim? Because the knife hadn't just slid from my hand, but shot across the room and lodged in my son's left thigh. We stared at each other. Bobby was so surprised he didn't cry out. Mouth agape, he just stared at me, a wad of half-chewed pancake crammed in his left cheek, as the wound went white before the blood rushed back, welled up, began to drip between us on the floor. It was quiet. The cat sat back. The baby watched. Outside, the landscapers put aside their edgers. Even the procession of morning traffic suddenly eased its inevitable parade by our home.

It wasn't until I heard the barrel of Ed's Royal typewriter ring upstairs, in fact, that we began to move again, trying to assume the roles we'd once portrayed like the costumes I suddenly perceived they were.

That's what I learned that day: a husband can become a monster; a son, a tragedy; a mother, a killer, in just an instant. That's all it takes for a new label to stick.

We are never quite who we think we are.

"Mom?" Bobby said. He was looking down at the hamhock of his left leg, at the knife, hilt-deep in his skin. The knife wobbled tenderly as he panted tiny iridescent gasps. Then with a yank—I tried to stop him—he pulled the blade out of his thigh.

Bobby has always been decisive. Just like his father.

"Stop!"

How long did it take me to move? Ten seconds? Twelve? Too long to rush to his side—to comfort him—to grab a batter-slick towel and bind his leg in a poor tourniquet that did little to abate the flow.

"Ed!" I'm sure I screamed. "For Christ's sake, Ed!"

There was no answer, and I had no time to coddle my reclusive husband from the half-light of his lair.

"Let's go," I said. Bobby stared at me blankly. "Your dad will meet us."

What else did I say? The words don't really matter. I know I kept a steady rap going to keep us focused (to keep *me* focused) as I moved him from the chair toward the car, then ran back inside for the baby. "Take my hand," I'm sure I told him as I pulled him upright. "That's right. Your arm on my waist. Now, all your weight on me." Finally we were hobbling toward the door: "That's just fine. You're doing great. Look how brave you are."

He was observing me with a singleness of attention that I hadn't felt since he was a tiny wrinkled pup curled in the crook of my arm.

"Mom?"

We were joined at the hip as we made our way to the car, but we were suddenly also connected in another, more profound, fashion, as though the knife that had broken his skin had penetrated other less permeable barriers—the ones between thoughts, between mother and son, between a child and himself.

"Mom," he was asking, "did I do something wrong? Why isn't Dad coming with us? Mom, why did you just call me Jules?"

In her car seat behind him, the baby burped, oblivious to the wreckage of her brother's leg, or the pain in my lungs. I could not breathe. I could not answer even one of Bobby's questions.

Sisters of Grace and Misericordia Hospital is only five miles from our home, and I had us there in an instant. How brave he was. Ashen-faced, he bit his lip as I, dressed only in my nightgown and robe, sped from the driveway—our old Volvo bottoming out as I drove the three of us over the curb. Bobby didn't even start to cry, in fact, until we arrived at the emergency room. He was in shock, the doctor later explained, and, until that moment, the episode wasn't quite real to him— probably because he knew I'd never hurt him, even "unconsciously," as the Board has proposed.

The Board doesn't know me well, even if we've met every other Wednesday at 8 a.m. for the past four months. I'm not one of those mothers who overstarches their children's clothes, or gives them bad haircuts, just to return, in some belated, unconscious way, the punishment of childbirth. I love my boy. It's that simple. And, at that moment, I wasn't yet fully aware of what had happened, not just to Bobby, but to our family as a whole.

But how could I have known my marriage was over? That Ed was to blame? That, soon, the baby wouldn't know me at all?

Why would I suspect my husband? Imagine he'd use words against me?

Even now, after all that has happened, I realize just how unhinged I sound. It's one thing to confess to your girlfriend over a glass of wine that your lover hurts you, treats you badly. Quite another to weep that he's cursed you, bewitched you—to claim your (now missing) husband controls your life and that every word he types comes true.

Who'd believe that?

Not even I believed that.

Not at first.

On the day Bobby was hurt, I only knew Ed was upstairs. Nowhere in sight.

Yet I'm now certain my husband made the knife leave my hands.

And that, for good measure, he then typed:

No one will ever believe you.

My dilemma is of an ancient Greek origin. Right, Cassandra?

Long story short: I'm screwed.

For his final act? Ed disappeared from my life.

After that day, I never saw my husband again.

Choke Box

On the "Dental Health" shelf of the BPI Library, there are innumerable illustrations of the mouth in all its disastrous salivary glory. Swollen tongues. Cancerous taste buds. Pustuled, deciduous gums. Enamel—cankered by moss, mud, hay. Lesions on the ventral tongue. Eruptions of the buccal or labial mucosa. At the tonsil, however, the filleted cross-sections suddenly stop. The throat, elegant in its architecture, has been censored: only a fringe of excised pages remains. Taunting L.E.T. readers like me who are interested only in self-improvement.

Fortunately, a "First Aid" manual fills in where the last image leaves off: a companion illustration wends its way down past the jaw, into the throat, and on toward the epiglottal cap where food and foreign objects have an "untoward predisposition" (so the pamphlet says) to "infelicitously" lodge themselves. Breathing: the epiglottis is wide open so air can pass through the trachea from mouth to lungs. Swallowing: it snaps shut so a cud of (I close my eyes, take a moment) roasted duck *en glace,* crisp rosemaried potatoes, and garlicked chard can slide its way down over the epiglottal shell into the esophagus, then the stomach below, like a drop of water over a turtle's back into a silent pond.

Talking, however, confuses the normally vigilant organ and, flapping open like a virgin's skirt, the epiglottis sends a mixed message of rejection and desire both—inviting a chaotic, unforgiving interlude. Naturally, the inevitable happens. A piece of food blocks the little hole. Breathing ceases. "Unless intervention occurs," the manual goes on, "respiratory cessation quickly follows."

Death, in short, is imminent.

The epiglottis may be the offending agent. But the voice box is to blame. The larynx creates sound, tone, pitch—gives meaning to every word the tongue tilts over the teeth. Yet its vibratory dissonance—the lingual crescendo that gives words their meaning—comes at a deadly price: the risk of death every time we eat and talk. No other species has the same problem. Oblivious, we live in danger. Until a hitch, a hiccup. And—then—it's too late.

Language is killing.

The manual puts it another way:

"Talking and eating—at the same time—is discouraged."

Fun Facts: Famous Chokers

Attila the Hun (barbarian ruler): 457 C.E. Offending agent: Nosebleed.

Cher (singer, actress, survivor): 1982. Offending agent: Vitamin pill.

George W. Bush (president, painter, survivor): 2002. Offending agent: Pretzel.

Mary Caponegro (writer, survivor): 1959. Offending agent: Safety pin.

Mama Cass (singer): 1974. Offending agent: Ham sandwich.

Tommy Dorsey (trombonist): 1956. Offending agent: Steak.

Carrie Fisher (actress, icon, survivor): 1980. Offending agent: Brussels sprout.

Jimmie Fox (baseball player): 1967. Offending agent: Chicken bone.

Jimi Hendrix (guitarist): 1970. Offending agent: Vomit.

Graydon Lesh (editor, writer, survivor): NA. Offending agent: Monocle.

Ramon Navarro (actor): 1968. Offending agent: Dildo.

Queen Mother (figurehead, survivor): 1993. Offending agent: Fishbone.

Ronald Reagan (president, actor, survivor): 1976. Offending agent: Peanut.

Tennessee Williams (playwright): 1983. Offending agent: Bottle cap.

CHAPTER THREE

The New Normal

Dr. McCready, the physician on call at Sisters of Grace and Misericordia Hospital, was an efficient sort who took one quick look at Bobby's leg and assured me at once that the knife had not hit an artery. While the blood loss was "significant," even "noteworthy," he went on (the staff mopping behind us), Bobby's injury required sutures. Not surgery. A crutch until the muscle healed.

My son would be fine. We both were safe.

There was nothing more to fear.

That's when I began to shake. Violently, I presume, since I was firmly directed into a chair by a sturdy mentholated woman in floral scrubs. As I collapsed, she made an odd, judgmental cluck with her tongue. A good mother, I inferred, could stand for her son if she loved him.

Mothers can be shamed in countless ways.

The nurse ignored the air of my humid defeat. As her facial hair caught the distressed glow of the lights, her pink eyes assessed with bored detachment Bobby's leg, my disarray, most of all Bobby's emerging grin (so very like him)—all this, as I stuttered and keened, rocked in my chair, beside him.

Bobby sighed. His overprotective mother was being a ninny. His baby sister was howling. Everything was normal again.

Normal. A word I haven't used in a long time.

"I'm all right, Mom," Bobby said, gritting his teeth as the doctor began to clean the wound gently. I rose and draped myself around him then—the nurse didn't even try to pull me off—and the two of us stayed that way until the doctor finished his grisly work.

Naturally, there were questions. The doctor asked how Bobby got hurt, I tried to explain, and it was only my own confusion, my son's peculiar cheerfulness, and the baby's contented farting as she kicked below us, still strapped in her car seat, that made him shrug off our small disaster as one of life's daily mysteries. He'd seen worse, he said. Not three months before, in fact, he'd pulled a nail from a carpenter's forehead: "a carpenter," he added, ruffling Bobby's sweat-matted hair, "who was wholly unaware the nail was there."

"A nail?" Of course my son at once perked up at a story involving potential gore.

"Right here." The doctor poked at a spot just above my son's left eye, and Bobby, distracted, began gently tapping his own forehead. Assessing its firmness. Like a melon's.

The nurse wheeled in a tray with an array of needles, sutures, and sponges, and I at once felt the fire at the top of my skull drain down the back of my throat. If McCready sensed my discomfort, however, he ignored it. While the nurse numbed Bobby with an impressively swift shot of Lidocaine, my son's attention remained on the good doctor and his story—just as he intended.

"What happened?" I asked. I didn't care. But, at that moment, it was my job to feign interest so Bobby wouldn't notice the gruesome tapestry his leg was becoming. I'm sure I was as white as a sheet. If I'd been a hot-air balloon, I would have sailed completely free of my moorings.

Later, the nurse used similar words at my ~~trial~~ (my "commitment hearing" Celeste corrects in the margins). The nurse said I looked "ghostly," as though I were "floating away."

"Do you mean to say," the judge asked, "that Mrs. Tamlin didn't seem *grounded?*"

I remember the way the nurse scratched her chin at that moment, shaking her head like a large dog after a nap, trying to imagine me hovering among the ER's air ducts, the dusty recessed lighting, as I looked down at my boy with his bloody leg stretched out on the table.

She tried to clarify. "That's not what I meant." Again the shake of her massive head. "Mrs. Tamlin looked scared," she said. More firmly now. "Terrified, even."

The judge still didn't get it: "Of what she'd done, you mean?"

The nurse sighed. And though Celeste intervened, helped the nurse explain that I seemed frightened and confused, not scared and guilty, the damage had been done.

I don't blame the nurse. My commitment wasn't her fault. Not one of us could have foreseen what was to come as Bobby lay on the table, his flesh peeled back, occasionally poking his numbed thigh as though it were a sodden plastic bag he'd fished from the tiny brook that burbled in our backyard.

"I can't feel it."

"Just like our carpenter friend," the doctor said, drawing Bobby's eyes up and away from the wound as he began his first stitch. "The carpenter was using a nail gun on roofing tiles before he climbed down to join his crew for lunch. And when he turned from his ladder . . . ," he paused, "his pals gagged in their tins when they saw the nail in his head."

Bobby was all ears as McCready leaned in toward him.

"The brain doesn't feel pain. Did you know that?"

Bobby didn't. Neither did I. McCready had an excellent bedside manner.

"Later, his pals decided the nail must have rebounded off the chimney's metal flashing before . . ." McCready pointed at his head with a gloved hand.

He smiled. "But he was lucky."

"Lucky?" Bobby was confused.

The doctor nodded as he sewed. "The nail embedded itself in a region of the brain that only controls short-term memory. In fact, that poor carpenter never remembered a thing about what happened that day, how the nail ended up in his head, even though he had a scar to prove it once was there." He looked up at my son as he continued to sew with quick even strokes. "It's too bad, really, since knowing what happened then . . . might have prevented what happened next."

"Next?" Bobby barely noticed as McCready knotted the final suture.

The doctor clucked. "Two months later, the carpenter showed up in the ER again," he coughed, "nailed in a far less bony region." He paused, sent a quick, conspiratorial look my way, then returned to admiring his work on Bobby's leg. "Let's just say, grownups can get caught up in all kinds of funny business." He bent to wrap some gauze over the wound. "But after the second accident, the police were pretty sure the first accident . . . wasn't an accident at all."

He sighed, shrugged. "They never got a chance to prove it though." His voice was far from the room, the bright lights above us.

"Why?" I winced, as he gave a final prod to his work.

Bobby's leg wept into the gauze from the pressure. But either the color or the amount of blood satisfied the doctor. He sat back, his hands limp in the air between us.

"The carpenter died from complications not long after." He

sighed. "I gather his second injury required elaborate . . ." He paused. ". . . reconstructive work."

His voice trailed off and he smiled at Bobby. "Whereas you, my friend," he said, "have nothing to worry about." With that, he snapped off his latex gloves, tossed them into a waiting can, and ruffled Bobby's hair.

"Wow." Bobby whistled softly.

As for me, what can I say? At that moment, I was grateful for the distraction of that poor carpenter's screwed-up love life.

Clearly, I'm a terrible woman.

The nurse grunted as she took the bowl of bloody pads away. McCready took one last look at his work, then picked up the butter knife. As he ran his fingers down the blade, it didn't escape any of us just how blunt it was. "Duller than a PTA meeting," I offered without much humor.

In retrospect, I should have chosen my words more carefully.

"We see a lot of crazy shit in the ER," McCready said drily, forgetting Bobby's age. Then he set the knife aside.

Picking up Bobby's chart, he started quickly checking boxes.

"Where is the father?" he asked, making a final note before he signed the record of his work.

"At his office," I said.

It wasn't precisely a lie.

CHAPTER FOUR

The Assertion

An experiment. I type six simple words:

"Everything my husband writes becomes true."

My assignment?

Verify this claim. For my children. The Board. Myself.

Even though it may be impossible.

But I will no longer deny, I can no longer deny:

What my husband writes on the page, now takes place near my person.

Wherever he is, Ed doesn't need to write a word.

Can you hear him?

He's laughing.

CHAPTER FIVE

Composition Axe

Compose yourself.

I repeat the words quietly. A silent instruction. A plea. A prayer.

See? I'm being composed.

But whose words are they? Mine? Or Ed's?

My husband laughs:

How can you tell?

Let me explain:

Not long after my husband began to write his book (from the first, he called it a "memoir"), I noticed an eerie correlation between scenes taking shape in his papers and odd incidents that began to occur in our home—as though Ed's solitary work at his desk upstairs was directly influencing our downstairs behavior. The effects were subtle at first. The cat went missing. Then my Volvo's transmission died. Later, the IRS showed up for an audit. Nothing unusual or extraordinary. Each event on its own merits was merely "inconvenient." Cats stray, after all. Cars die. Is it surprising that I at first believed that the sudden abundance of ill-timed events in our lives was no more uncommon than a hair clot in a bath drain? A temporary obstruction that—with the right tools, a bit of patience—was entirely resolvable? I'll admit I was slow on the uptake. It took me much too long to see the connection between my husband's work and our daily troubles, and, by then, as with most things in marriage, it was much too late to stop what was happening from spiraling out of control.

For once I think my mother was right: the most dangerous place a woman can be is in the so-called "safety" of her home. The statistics don't prove her wrong.

I'm aware that my "explanation" (the Review Board at Buffalo Psychiatric has pressed me to call it a "confession") won't satisfy the committee of six that is responsible for overseeing the small discretionary movements I once controlled myself. They're a humorless lot—huddled and scoliotic in their mismatched plastic chairs. Yet for all their oily cynicism, they've never ignored me, never lied to me. Never even raised their voices during our dreaded, biweekly meetings. True, they're hard to fathom, to get a rise out of. But at least—at the very *least*—they are reliable. That's more than I can say of my family. Certainly of Ed.

At night, when the hall lights dim (they never go fully dark here), and my most morbid thoughts surge against the rising chemical swell of my last Dixie-cup dosage, I fear I've come to find the Board's unflagging equilibrium so soothing that I must have changed as irrevocably as they accuse. After all, they don't nag or bicker. They don't lash out. They don't even roll their eyes at my (admittedly) snide assessments of their limitations: the ill-fitting suits, the mottled, over-fluoresced skin, the predictable short-sightedness in vision as much as intellect. To them, I'm just one case among so many others, and they've heard enough lies and exhortations—from small fibs to outright rants—to make them stony and steadfast, as if rigor mortis were a condition they've become as accustomed to sporting as the tweed coats with patched elbows they all like to wear. Under any other circumstances, I might have respected their dour commitment. (I have a helpless and embarrassing admiration for authority figures.) But when someone like me comes along—educated, devoted, and, truly, still somewhat naïve after all that has happened—it's evident they're at a loss. They've already decided that my behavior is an act.

My story? A desperate woman's fabrication.

"You've read the statistics on domestic violence?" anonymous Board Member 4 asks, for instance, referring to the pamphlet he'd given me at our last "progress" hearing. When I nod but then go on to explain (once again, I might add) that I did not kill my husband of ten years—that Ed simply disappeared—he sighs a great breathy chortle that shakes phlegm from his jowls. His meaning is clear: I remain a source of great disappointment to him. If only I'd admit what I've done, he'd finally be happy: they'd *all* be happy.

What he really means is that they all could go home.

Board Member 6 chimes in. His hair is short, his glasses large. He wears woolen trousers even in the unbearable summer heat.

"Do you miss your husband?" Beneath his question is a subtext with which I've become all too familiar.

"Of course," I retort. "We were a happy family. At least," I say, "until Ed started writing that book."

"And then?"

"And then," I say, "it was as if Ed had left us."

"You mean," he says, his eyes on my file, "that he *died*." With greater emphasis now: "That you *killed* him."

He levies this insult without once looking up from his notes.

"I mean," I say more firmly, "that he *disappeared*."

I get flustered. Anyone but a murderer would in the face of such blunt accusations. Fortunately, my counselor steps in on my behalf.

"As the Board well knows," she says politely in her light, carefully childlike voice, "Edward Tamlin hasn't yet been located."

"True enough," BM4 jumps back in, his fleshy nose quivering over my file. "But that's precisely why we're here."

With a unified nod, they break for lunch, naturally without consulting me. They will decide my fate in the town nearby over seared mahi mahi and pinot noir or a ribeye steak and a nice rioja. But I already know what their verdict will be. I can see it in my counselor Celeste's face: Celeste—such a sweet girl—who has, from the first, fought for me harder than anyone else. Even my own family.

It was at her request that I began to write what she calls my "counter-memoir." I resisted at first. I'd had enough of authors and books, the queer energy that Ed's work had led to. But with Celeste's encouragement—not to mention the pen and paper she regularly smuggled into my room during her consultations—I relented. Ed, after all, was no longer around to correct his book about our marriage and his life before we met. And while the memoir he wrote—incomplete at the time of his disappearance—will never see the light of day as long as I refuse to sign the release forms Celeste delivered to me, I also learned long ago that lawyers have a nasty habit of worming their way through even the tiniest loopholes. They'd never allow an alleged murderess like me to stand in the way of their share of a profit. So here I am: composing myself. Steeling myself against a book that has changed the shape of my family: a memoir that took Ed away, sent my children down state. A book that managed to get me locked up without cause. ("Civil commitment," Celeste corrects again.) All that before it's even in print.

At the time of this writing, my motives aren't yet wholly clear to myself. Naturally, I'd like my side of this story to be heard. I'll even admit I crave recognition for my efforts on behalf of my children, my brother. Even my husband. But I've learned enough in the past year to know that airing one's dirty laundry on a line doesn't make it any cleaner: it just elevates its altitude. And, really, what good is that?

What I truly desire is what all mothers desire: for my children to understand me. For my children to one day realize the full extent of what occurred in our home. How I was led astray by love. Done in by betrayal. And—finally—ruined by the peculiar "factors" (what else can I call them?) that altered my admittedly incomplete understanding of natural laws. Not to mention, my relations with Ed.

Perhaps—if I'm lucky, if I get this story straight—my memory of those missing six seconds will at last return. I'll finally know what went down at the farmhouse. And maybe? What the future holds for me too.

Of course the cynic in me whispers something much different. More dire. A warning that even now is hard to write down, as I just now have, since it once was so easy for me to have faith—to *believe*—in the simple life I was living:

Women, don't trust the men in your lives.

And trust the women even less.

CHAPTER SIX

Moving the Lines

The six men on the Board at Buffalo Psychiatric are aware that poor memory—what they prefer to call "selective amnesia"—is often the result of trauma. But like old dogs digging for bones in the wrong yard, they just won't let my case go. Instead, they regard my behavior as entirely deliberate, even though Dr. McCready has sworn ("to God and the equal powers of New York State") that the butter knife incident was inexplicable: the blade was much too blunt to cause the injury on Bobby's leg. How it came to lodge in my son's left thigh without collateral damage (bruising or so-called "hesitation strikes") completely baffled him. At my hearing, he called the injury "a freak accident." (The attending nurse called it an "act of God.") Even I didn't know what to think back then. By the time Bobby's leg had healed, however, I was sure the blame was Ed's.

Ed tried to hurt our son.

About this, I have no doubts.

The Board will say that Ed didn't hurl the knife. That it's unlikely he even heard our old Volvo gasp down the driveway as I throttled the clutch toward the ER. In fact, they've reminded me that I heard him working in his office upstairs—that the typewriter rang as I ran out the door, leaving a trail of blood behind me. I've never disputed the timeline they offer. There's just more to the story. Layers. The Board senses that: I suspect it's why they're so darn testy with me. But seeing the bottom of a well and knowing it's there are much different matters. The latter requires imagination. The former, just a length of rope and a good set of eyes.

For this story, the Board needs both.

By all appearances, Bobby's injury that April morning set into motion a peculiar chain of events: the audit. The baby's injury. Not long after, the fire. Finally, the restraining order.

Three months later? All hell broke loose.

And now Buffalo Psychiatric is my home.

If you think that's the sum of my story, though, reconsider. This is Ed's story as told by (through?) me, his wife, Jane Marie Tamlin—just one of the many "characters" in his "memoir" over whom he continues to exert control. It might be said that this book—the one I'm writing now at Celeste's urging—is a companion text to Ed's unpublished work. Its goal: to refute Ed's claims, the allegations about me and our family.

To snap my fingers and dispel the trance.

The teller always changes the tale. Ed was a lawyer: he knew that. Words lead to actions; words make events happen. There is a direct correlation. Always. Even if it's difficult at first to see.

So I will tell this tale. All of it. Ed's infidelity. My mother's betrayal. My young brother's "career" at my expense.

Yet my goal isn't blame.

My mission is change. To correct Ed's story.

My hope? That these words—scratched in the dark and in secret—bring light.

Mine is a pedestrian task: there is no joy in revision. No excitement in setting a story straight. Like keeping a child from straying into the street, my job is merely minding the curb. But if it's a mother's job to set limits, keep order, then I'm up to the task. Only I can explain how my husband's book changed my family's life. Only I can expose Ed for being a liar so I can prove I'm telling the truth.

It hasn't escaped me that this *counter-memoir* serves as a defense for a woman who has already been judged. It's the kind of ironic plot twist over which Ed would gloat if he still were with us. In fact, I wouldn't be surprised to learn he's the cruel arbiter of its construction. That, even now, I remain the ventriloquist's dummy, Ed's fist at the base of my spine.

So the question is: Can a dummy talk when her operator isn't around?

Answer: Is it possible to prove otherwise?

For my part, I've come to believe the dummy is telling her story. Too often we're just listening with indifferent ears.

For the sake of this memoir, then, I will suppose that I'm free to speak. That my words are my own.

Sticks and stones may break my bones. But I will go on as if words can help me.

Can you see my problem? Are those Ed's words? Or my own?

Is it surprising that even now I believe my husband wields a power over me? A sane woman would never say such things. Yet dogs respond to frequencies outside human perception. We train them to it. That's how it is with Ed and me. He seems to have been gone for one year (at least according to the official record). Nevertheless, I can still sense him. I can feel him at his corrosive work, composing our lives, changing our days, hemming me into this sterile place with its plastic forks and worn linoleum so that I can't interfere with what, not long before his disappearance, he described to me—the proud mother of his (now) eleven-year-old son and (almost) two-year-old daughter—as his "single most important work."

So if most people believe that this story begins with the butter knife incident, I'm happy to oblige them. It's a convenient introduction into my strange life.

But then, as I've already admitted, even I'm not wholly sure what happened that April day in my kitchen.

The only person who *really* knows is Ed.

CHAPTER SEVEN

Equations of Loss

The ride home from the ER that April afternoon was so slow and steady that it was easy to forget our frantic rush there a few hours before. I took my time, rolling to a stop at each yellow light as other cars sped by me. We waved to bikers and pedestrians, counted birds on wires. Bobby spoke in half sentences when he spoke at all—and I replied with an array of gestures. In her car seat, the baby yawned, kicked, but didn't complain. The three of us sank back into the plush mattress of daily life together as if it were made from a warm loaf of fresh bread. We must have still been in shock.

At the pharmacy, the pace picked up again as we studied boxes of bandages and antiseptic creams under the fluorescent lights. The small differences in their ingredients mattered greatly to us: we dithered and argued. Beside me, Bobby limped down the overwaxed aisle floors, careening as he worked his new crutches. While in the stroller, the baby grew impatient, reached out, knocked bottles of pills off shelves. The other shoppers took in my cinched, blood-spattered bathrobe and shimmied out of our way, their glances brusque, accusatory. When I caught a guard watching us in the security mirror, I smiled. But as soon as he turned, my pent-up fury swallowed me whole: I gave him the finger. Then stuffed a family-sized bag of M&Ms into my purse.

In a rare turn of good fortune that security footage has never come to light.

There was something I needed to say to Bobby. I could feel it rising beneath my ribs, words that could cut to the heart of what had happened that morning, salve the wound between us, the one we'd neglected while we tended his leg. The syllables were hard, carbuncular, at the back of my throat. They dug into my uvula, my tonsils. Scraped the root of my tongue. If only I could spit them out.

Instead, I coughed a chalky kernel of dried phlegm into my fist.

At that moment, I did the worst possible thing you could do to a boy. (Even now, I reproach myself.) As we stood in line to cash out, I took Bobby's hand, held it over my heart. In front of a cast of other shoppers in various shades of undress, I told him I loved him. I couldn't wait a moment longer. (My therapist calls it as a "self-ulcerating pathology.") And my embarrassed, overmedicated tween son's response was totally predictable. He pushed me away. Snapped at me to stop. Then, as I reached for him—as he tried to bolt out of reach—he stepped back, tripped over his crutch; and when I, in synchrony, stepped forward, reaching out to steady him, my own foot snagged the wheel of the stroller. Suddenly, as boxes of gauze flew into the air all around us, we were tumbling together—*ass over elbow*, as Ed likes to say—onto the pharmacy's worn linoleum. Before we could right ourselves, the shopper behind us took our place in line. In a snap, he was off, a forty-ounce bottle of Schlitz and a jar of antacids tucked neatly under one arm.

It was all too much for Bobby: his eyes flashed as the baby started to howl. With a gritty, jaw-grinding bark, he scrambled up as best he could and, like a broken bird, hobbled away, dragging his crutch behind him. Outside, I could see him hunched by the glass doors where the drunks, on similarly unsteady legs, usually begged for change.

It only takes a moment to sever a new connection, and I'd destroyed the one we'd shared at the ER in even less time. From then on, there was a shadow around Bobby, a phantom boy waiting to step in, take over. I recognized him by the thrust of his chin. In the bloodless recession beneath his eyes. This boy was stronger. More dour. Like his father, stern and edgy. He was, I realized, the young man Bobby would soon become—a boy who continued to resemble me, but who would, in no time at all, become as unyielding as the man I had married.

He was a boy in the future tense.

I knew Bobby would forgive me. But he wouldn't forget what had happened. Instead, like Ed, he would calculate. Plot.

"Injury has value," my lawyer-husband once said. "It's only *how much* that's ever in question." Bobby had heard that lecture as often as I had.

This is the equation of loss. Every day, I began to lose my son a bit more as the new boy grew in his place, accumulated mass, took my child over. Sure, Bobby played patient for me, laughed at my awkward jokes, at the small gifts I left at his side while he drowsed under the influence of his junior strength narcotics: there was a new bell for his bike, a pocket flashlight, a book of optical illusions. Yet each time he thanked me sweetly, I could feel the other boy calculating the algorithm of guilt that had developed between us: the ongoing differential in our behavior from the moment the butter knife flew across the room. The old Bobby looked straight ahead, barely noticed when I left a plate of cookies on the table beside him. The new Bobby kept me lined up in his peripheral vision, always watched from the sides of his eyes. There was never any going back. We'd already begun to move forward—further away—from the people we'd once been.

Practically speaking, that meant I gave in to the old Bobby's every request. He borrowed my cell phone whenever and for however long he wished. Though I winced when he bragged, not far enough out of earshot, about the stabbing to his friends.

Josh wanted to come over to see his leg. Cedric too.

"Please?" Bobby was remarkably polite. Unusually so.

Perhaps he was in fear of you? The Board always asks this question.

Nonsense, I say. *My boy has always known—he still knows—I love him.*

"They can come this weekend," I promised.

It was a few days away, but Bobby didn't ask again. Perhaps he knew he needed time to heal. Or sensed what was about to happen—that his entire world was about to change. I'll never know. He won't tell me now. Not since my mother took him away, stuffed his head with mothballs and straw, made him stupid with her stories about me. The velvet scent of her hair. The delicate paper of her patchouli skin. My mother's lies are infectious, she can send people reeling. I can't expect her own grandson—soon her ward—to have the skill to doubt her.

I try not to think of the baby. Her tender thighs, her warm breath. How her eyes, her mouth, first searched for me. We were magical, the three of us. But what can she remember of her mother after all this time?

I try to stay confident. Back then, after all, Bobby was his impish self in no time at all. Can't that happen again?

On Saturday morning, his friend Josh arrived as planned.

"Look where my mom cut me," he bragged, thrusting his leg out and peeling back the enormous new gauze pad I'd taped over the slowly scabbing stitches. Bobby was leaning much harder on his crutch than he needed to (his pain medication took off the edge), and he gasped theatrically as he revealed the wound for a cursory inspection. I winced as Josh prodded Bobby's leg: the meat of his thigh was now puckered and raw. But Bobby smiled as Josh bent and sniffed the stitches. They were two small dogs, pup teeth primed and ready, circling each other; their hind legs taut, skittery, working out who was boss.

"Wow." Josh whistled and nudged his friend.

Bobby's smile was all I needed to get through the rest of the day.

Before long, they wandered off to the narrow stream in our backyard. Normally, they would have hunted for frogs in the moss-covered rocks, leaping from one stone to the next, splashing in the marshy grass until their sneakers were covered in the fetid sludge from which life, as we know it, first crawled.

When they returned, however, their sneakers were dry. Bobby had remained on the banks because he couldn't bend over.

I'd never realized just how sad a sight two spotless boys could be.

The ragged crusts that formed quickly over Bobby's wound— a cipher of dried blood and torn muscle—soon became the first hesitant scratchings of a story sutured right onto his skin. When his friends stopped by, perhaps a guest, or an unlucky neighbor—pretty much anyone who passed us by— Bobby would at once point to his leg and, without fail, begin a sweeping oratory, reiterating (without disclaimers) the unbelievable saga of that day's events, always beginning with the same studied words: *Who knows what happened in the kitchen that morning? I remember where I was sitting. Even what I was eating before I got cut. But how one thing led to the other? I only remember that I was hungry. Then Mom was crying. The baby puke♦ on the floor. An♦ the cat began sniffing my leg.*

Soon everyone—from the postman to the principal—knew what had happened over pancakes that ill-fated morning, and the look of horror that swept over my face when Bobby began his predictable journey down memory lane soon became an inflated performance rivaling Bobby's coddled account. After all, he didn't need a mother when his friends came calling. He needed a showgirl, a lovely assistant, to frame his tale. A forty-three-year-old housewife in brown corduroys and a stained t-shirt wasn't much. So I brushed my hair. Bought a new dress. Started doing a few sit-ups at night.

I would have done anything to re-win his trust.

"Crocodile tears," my neighbor Joy Westin (whose home sat at three o'clock on the neighborhood circle) later testified. My revulsion, she claimed, seemed a "pretense." My dismay, "a bad act."

Yet how many times could I hear Bobby's story—in all its appalling detail—and still look shocked? No matter how I first had felt.

In any case, Joy, it turns out, was a better actress than I was. Much better. She proved that at my hearing.

Joy's a cunt. Celeste's margin commentary. Or is that mine? Sometimes our writing looks oddly alike.

The simple fact is that I never thought my horror was in doubt, a naïveté that leaves me breathless now. How could anyone doubt my love? My story?

Do you doubt the air? Your own breath?

I am Bobby's mother. Our relation is infinite. Impermeable. From the moment I felt his first stirrings inside me, "I" knew "I" wasn't "I" any longer. "I" was someone else, a surplus of identity: there was no accounting, suddenly, of how much me "I" could become as his fetal tail rippled against my uterine wall, jostling in turn my subcutaneous tissues (an unsettling tickle that couldn't be scratched or arrested) so that, whoever "I" once might have been, "I" could never be "me" again. Soon: the pulse of his hand was pressing hard against mine as he reached out, palm to palm, into a universe of stippled, overstretched belly. Soon: the kicks, the elbowed demands. Then, at last, the infant himself, bruised and snorting in disbelief at the sterile, over-oxygenated air of the hospital's hot delivery room.

The day Bobby was born, he didn't just pass from womb into world, from the cool, loamy woods to our furnished yard. He'd taken a part of me along in that journey, left me a kicked up genetic froth, a puzzle rearranged. A mother dies a little each time a child is born, and I tended the sweet infant mewls and growled demands with diligent and desperate care, not because I loved Bobby (though I did). But because Bobby *was* me. My blood and bone cosmology. I hadn't just given him my fabled rib. But the calcium in my teeth. The iron in my blood. The curvature of my corneas. I felt him— still feel him—the same way I ached from a crick in my leg that woke me at night. My atoms flickered, fired up in their new body home. Blood called out to blood.

Perhaps that's why some mothers lose their way. Kill their children. As though they can get back what they've lost—or at least sever the tie—become satisfyingly finite again. But the filicide is an optimist. She believes the future can be changed. Whereas most mothers live in a state of simple anguish that, to our rewired brains, feels like joy.

You can call it despair. It still feels good. Ask any addict.

Instead, let me pose this question to the Board: what would have been left of "me" if "I'd" done "him" in as, scrawny legs swinging, Bobby sat at our table slicing up pancakes and cramming them gleefully into his mouth?

How could "I" have gone on?

During her cross-examination, Celeste did her best to put Joy in her place, to stem the tide of bad news.

"You know Jane Tamlin well?" she asked Joy almost off-handedly.

One overstuffed shoulder pad twitched. A mild spasm crossed my neighbor's jaw.

"We have mutual friends."

Celeste nodded. "You must have heard about Bobby's injury the day it happened, then?"

As it turned out, Joy had found out about Bobby's trip to the ER two days after we'd sped down the driveway—an eon, Celeste argued, in "neighborhood gossip" time. But none of that mattered to the sour, childless judge overseeing Joy's testimony. He couldn't see that her neighborliness, like her parental devotion, was merely an act; that her kids spent all their time at friends' homes and summer camps. Joy's posture was invincible.

"A good mother," she opined with appalling conviction, "always feels her kids' pain." She tapped an immaculate heel. "No matter what."

This is the face of irony: Joy Westin mouthing words I have said in her impeccably tailored Burberry suit. Joy Westin acting like me . . . much better than I ever could. Yet no one could see it.

"Ask her if she had an epidural," I cranked at Celeste during our short recess later. "Did she feel her kids' pain then too?"

I am nothing if not contrary.

"A good mother," Celeste chirped, "is never snide."

Celeste was smiling, but there was pain in her voice.

Joy Westin had damaged our case. No two ways about it.

Blood Choke vs. Air Choke

In martial arts, a distinction is drawn between two different types of chokeholds: a "blood choke," which puts pressure on the carotid arteries or jugular veins, interfering with the flow of blood to the brain; and an "air choke," which compresses the trachea, prevents breathing, and leads to air hunger.

If done properly, blood chokes are temporary and very fast-acting. Subdued victims typically lose consciousness in a matter of seconds.

By contrast, an air choke, can be painful and take up to two minutes to perform. It may also cause trauma to the larynx or hyoid bone.

While both methods can subdue or kill, the blood choke also yields the potential for sexual pleasure (*see: erotic and auto-erotic asphyxiation*).

"Burking" is an unrelated form of air choke invented in 1827 by the murderers William Burke and William Hare, who smothered sixteen victims during the West Port murders. In order to create a lucrative supply of cadavers for medical schools (which required specimens without visible injuries), Burke and Hare sat on and compressed their victims' chests while covering the victims' noses and mouths with their hands.

In common parlance today? "Burking" now means "to quietly suppress."

Partial List of Chokeholds
Anaconda Choke
Gator Roll Choke
The Peruvian Necktie
Rear Naked Choke
Drop Dead Choke
Ezekiel Choke
Arm Triangle Choke
Regina Choke
Guillotine Choke
Triangle Choke
North South Choke
Push Choke

CHAPTER EIGHT

The Knife, the Scar, the Rat

Like any child, Bobby picked at the scabs that formed on his leg. Lost in thought, he'd flick bits of them out into the living room ether as if the outdated green shag carpet there could germinate the cured bits of leg meat like pollinating seeds. As he sat there—mossy and medicated in his nest on the couch—I found it easy to imagine a forest of limbs sprouting from the seedlings around him: a bushy scrub of tube-socked and knobby-armed flora swaying mildly beneath the cracked plaster ceiling.

Perhaps it helped that I was double-dosing his Vicodin. One for him, one for me. Just for a few days to take off the edge. No harm done.

I'm sure the wound was itchy: all that scratching and picking was predictable. But as the days wore on and Bobby returned to school, it soon became clear that his "unconscious habit" was in fact a purposeful intervention. Bobby was working the wound. Keeping it tender and primed in a state of irritated ooze. The injury had evidently brought him celebrity at Harris Hill. So, he reasoned, he'd make the wound look worse. Keep it raw. Jagged. Flashing it to his fourth-grade homeroom, he'd (once again) tell the story about how I stabbed him. How he "barely survived." How the doctors (all of them) sewed him back together without giving him "euthanasia."

When an infection set in, the pus welling up like old clotted milk, Bobby was elated. I called him on it. He just shrugged.

"Even Jimmy Hammond doesn't hassle me now," he said.

Apparently, Bobby had told his "friend" that my knife-wielding days were "just beginning." I tried not to groan as he laughed.

"Don't let her fool you," Bobby told Jimmy. "She's tougher than she looks."

Tough. What can my son think of me now?

There's a note in the margins here from Celeste. *Do you really think,* she's written, *that Bobby would love you more if he believed you were . . .* (a word or words crossed out) *. . . dangerous?*

Our case wasn't going well. Normally, she wouldn't ask such direct questions.

"It would be nice," I tell her when we meet two days later, "if I was as powerful as Bobby imagines." I pause, reformulate the thought. "I want Bobby to believe I *am* powerful. That's not quite the same thing."

Celeste smiles, squeezes my arm. It's so rare to be touched. "Is nuance prudent in a memoir? You sound like you're hedging." She tries a stronger word. "Lying." Now a wave of one hand as if she's batting a fly. "Let's just keep all that complexity to ourselves."

"Isn't life complicated?" I say.

I sound more tense than I'd like.

She shrugs. "But a good story isn't. See the difference?"

It's reasonable advice. But it's not right. I tell her as much.

She sighs. "Jane, I think you already know that what is 'correct' and what is 'advisable' are not the same thing."

In the hall outside the meeting room, the chatter rises and recedes as patients and nurses pass by my door.

"Don't forget," Celeste adds, "we're presenting your 'story,' not your 'life.' If I can't make your case easy on the ears . . ." She trails off, she doesn't need to say any more.

Celeste tries to look stern; it's hard for her. She is a slim twenty-eight. Her glossy hair neatly frames her face in loose waves. It's impossible for her to look weighty or severe. She's smart, of course. But I'm counting more than I'd like to admit on her looks: that the Board will want to keep her talking, take added interest in my case. That's not a gamble. Or a chauvinism. That's strategy. (A check here in the margins from Celeste: evidently she agrees.)

So I nod, pretend to listen. But what Celeste doesn't seem to understand—who really could?—is that, since Ed started writing his memoir, the so-called "presentation" of my life had *become* my life. The results are more apparent if you glance at my file. I read like a caricature. A send-up. A literary type on a downward spiral: overtaxed mother; madwoman in the attic; murderess. It's exhausting: I'm so much more.

But that's much, much too complicated, as Celeste would say. Grit your teeth, I remind myself, hunker down. Act simple, true. Don't ask questions. Or complain. Be the sad, misunderstood woman your attorney has asked you to be.

Be a woman she can defend.

Tell the story about Bobby's face-off with Jimmy, Celeste writes in the margins. *No U-turns or double axels. Keep it simple. Shoot straight. Charm us.*

Right.

First, set the stage. Introduce the characters: two "tween" boys. One large, the other small. Both wear clothes that don't fit well. They're growing too quickly: one up, the other out. The place: the second-floor hallway of Harris Hill Elementary. The smells: disinfectant, baby powder, corn syrup, stale bread. The light: diffuse. The sounds: muffled voices, the squeak of steel on linoleum, the faint buzz of fluorescent lights. Blackboard chalk crushed beneath heels. The weather: cloudy with a chance of impetuous play.

SIMPLE. This time she's underlined it.

Then: *Don't get cute.*

I obey.

Jimmy couldn't resist targeting a skinny boy with a limp. When he saw Bobby hobbling down the hall at Harris Hill two weeks after his "friend" was stabbed, Jimmy didn't care that he'd just been to see Principal Deng for a lunchroom violation. He crossed the hall at once, got in Bobby's way. He didn't push Bobby. Just used his big body to block my son's path. With a nudge of one prehistoric hip, he toppled Bobby into the lockers.

By then, Bobby was using a cane, and the wound looked like a rotting mushroom from his careful "attentions." The pus was pink, a curdled bloom at the center. Brown and florid near the rim. The gash itself was slimy and smelled like sweaty feet.

Jimmy pointed at a bulge in the deepest pocket of Bobby's cargo pants.

"Give it," he said. He probably thought it was a cell phone. Or cash.

Jimmy got what he asked for. Bobby pulled the butter knife out, held it up for Jimmy to see. Maybe he pointed it at Jimmy's gut. Or the pulse in his neck. Maybe directly at his eyes.

"To give Jimmy," he said with a shrug, "a better look."

Even hours later, the trace of an unfortunate twinkle still lit up his eyes as he relayed the story in our kitchen.

Let me point out that I last saw the butter knife in the ER when Dr. McCready rinsed Bobby's blood off the blade. I had no idea my son had taken it.

Evidently Jimmy was impressed. "Cool," he said, reaching out. "Is it sharp?"

Bobby smirked. "My mom stabbed me with it." He was the picture of tween casual. "Look," he added, unbuckling his belt and letting his pants fall over one hip to show the gash.

Enter Bobby's history teacher, a lukewarm mug of a man balancing a bruised banana on a stack of folders. He was in a rush, and when he turned the corner late for class, he only saw the butter knife and Bobby's half-bare ass. What he thought was going on out in a public hallway I'll never know. But I've been told the students heard his sputter and squeal all the way to the other end of the school.

Until the following day, butter knives weren't addressed in Harris Hill Elementary's student bylaws. Nonetheless, I received a call on my cell phone shortly after the incident to "retrieve" Bobby from the principal's office at once. They'd "confiscated a weapon," the excited secretary said, her voice full of bubble and mush.

That the school disposed of the knife, or lost it, has been a blow to my defense. No one, save the boys and McCready, believes just how blunt the blade really was. Alas, a boy's impression is rarely trusted. As for McCready, Celeste recently found out he's a recovered drunk. And though that's one step better than a "practicing" drunk, "any description," she said, "with the word 'drunk' in it, quite simply, is a problem."

The nurse backed me up, of course. But when it later came out that she and McCready enjoyed a regular supply-closet tryst, her testimony held as much weight as the wind.

The breadth of my misfortune still gives Celeste pause. (It's why, she tells me, she took on my case.) Even the Board senses something is fishy, I hear. But, like everyone else, they think I'm the rotting carp in the basket of daisies. Not my dear missing husband, Ed.

I'll admit it: I made a scene that afternoon in the principal's office, grounding Bobby right then and there—for a week! without screen time! without your phone!—ignoring the teachers and students passing by in the halls. And not long after, Bobby returned the favor. A new hand signal was making the rounds at Harris Hill, he said, smirking. All the kids were doing it: a wave that ended as a covert chop to the neck. "Dedicated to all crazed moms." He gave me a long look then. And I didn't want to hear any more.

One good thing came of that day: Jimmy Hammond stopped bullying Bobby. In fact, from then on, they became friends the way coyotes are friendly. Looking out for each other while they're both strong. Just waiting to see who will weaken first. Patient for an opportunity to pounce.

What the School Board called Bobby's "threatening behavior" was nothing more than childish high jinks. Still, they ordered Principal Deng to investigate. I should have suggested they also look into Jimmy's behavior; but given the so-called "peril" I'd recently posed to my son, I instead dutifully attended the "emergency meeting" to which I was summoned and explained—demurely and in as much detail as I could muster (good practice for recent days)—what had happened in our kitchen three weeks prior. Which is to say, I tried to explain what had preceded Bobby's actions with Jimmy, or, as the school board put it: what made Bobby "act out."

Naturally, I didn't tell the school board what *really* took place, what (that is) I began to *suspect* took place. How Ed was involved. I was already under the impression that the truth, *my* truth, would complicate matters.

So I apologized.

I sighed earnest gusts of wind.

I promised to monitor "my son's behavior" more closely.

It was only later that I realized that no one had asked why Ed hadn't accompanied me to the meeting. Principal Deng and his school board allies had just assumed my husband was busy at work. And mothers—*good* mothers, that is—even working mothers, are always free.

As for Ed, he was busy, of course. Just not at his law firm. Not at any job per se. At all.

Even Regina Hammond and I came to some sort of understanding later that week—in my kitchen during our scheduled "Conciliation Event," making up (paradoxically enough) in the same spot in my home where the trouble began, while our sons rummaged outside in the yard. Principal Deng even praised the reports we wrote at the school board's request. As he sat at his desk—Regina and I across from him, the history teacher pacing his orthopedic shoes out in the hall—Deng closed Bobby's file with unnecessarily dramatic flair.

The fluorescent lights glinted off the principal's shiny, pocked scalp. He looked weary but satisfied.

"It's time," he nodded, "we all moved on."

I was relieved, even happy, to put the incident behind me. If I instinctively pushed my chair back when Deng leaned across the desk to shake my hand, it was only because his renowned bad breath radiated the gritty bouquet of the future: the death that awaits us all.

I breathed through my mouth, leaned forward, and took his moist hand firmly in my own.

"This matter," he said, "is now closed."

If only that had been true.

Of course I was pleased we'd put the matter to bed. Until it occurred to me as I was driving home from his office that axioms that refer to closure always leave a small opening—the probability, really—of a return. What's been put to bed eventually reawakens; don't we let sleeping dogs lie because, if they're startled awake, they'll bite?

If there's implied danger, a threat, within every truce, what good is a truce at all?

It had been much too easy to appease Regina. She should have been shrill, demanding. At least edgy. *My* son, after all, had pointed a knife at *her* son. Yet she walked easily into my kitchen for our Conciliation Event as if the situation—or perhaps the place—was familiar.

Turns out it was both. But I didn't know that yet.

Regina sat down at the table, in the same seat Bobby had taken on that unfortunate April morning. She seemed calm. Almost relaxed.

"Boys. Look at them." She gestured toward the window, showing off her perfect manicure as our boys ran outside in the grass.

I nodded and quickly tucked my own hands under the table so she couldn't see them. My knuckles were blue, the flesh loose and veiny. I often bit my nails down to the rind.

I tried to adopt her tone.

"So much fuss," I sighed.

Regina was watching Jimmy through the window as he pressed Bobby's face into a wet pile of leaves. I didn't say anything—nor did she a moment later when Bobby elbowed Jimmy hard in the gut. There was a brief scuffle, some dirt flew, and then suddenly the boys were hobbling and laughing, throwing handfuls of sod at each other. I wondered if it was just an act, if they knew we were watching. I wondered if Regina thought the same thing.

"Fortunately, it's over now," I said.

"Yes." She inflected the simple word with derision. Yet, as she studied the boys, her eyes betrayed another, more complex emotion—something like envy, I thought. As though she wished she knew where her own butter knife was, how sharp it might be, and to what other uses it might be applied.

With a flip of her bob, however, the moment passed, and she pulled a prop from her oversized purse: a catalog she'd just discovered, she said. She thought I might like it.

"How nice," I said. Though I was more than confused.

She paused, considered, her finger coming to rest on the "Papa Hemingway Porch Rocker series" trimmed in a "hardy Floridian cane."

She tilted her head, and her hair tumbled over one shoulder elegantly.

"Ed would go for that, I bet."

"Ed?" I'm sure I looked surprised.

"Isn't he the writer in the family?"

I had to compose myself. I had no idea he'd told anyone about his memoir.

"That's what he tells me," I smiled.

Back then, I still tried to conceal the weariness I already felt, but it took a great deal of energy to sound nonchalant.

Regina laughed. "From what he says, it seems like it's going well."

What a rat. This from Celeste in the margins. Sometimes I could just kiss her.

Ed must have mentioned the book to Regina in passing. Perhaps while at one of our neighbor's parties after Bobby and I had gone to bed. I'd become a recluse while I was pregnant (it's awkward to chat poolside when you've got someone swimming inside you), and if he had told anyone, it would have been her. Regina, after all, liked to advertise the range and breadth of her education: her BA in communications from Union College (where she'd met Bernard at a mixer), had been followed by an MA in English at Buffalo State. She'd completed her coursework, but then "James" (as she liked to call her brute of a son) "came along" and she'd never finished her thesis "on fruit bowls," she once told me, "in Virginia Woolf's fiction." Regina coughed. "You know, she was the Martha Stewart of her day. Writer. Chef. Designer. Think of all the product lines." Regina tossed her head. "She asked for a room and five hundred pounds a year. But she knew she was worth much, much more. And when she didn't get it, *poof.*"

I assumed "poof" referred to Woolf's suicide. But as we nibbled cheese from the plate of hors d'oeuvres I'd set out, it seemed best not to ask.

Regina dabbed at her lips with a napkin, took a sip of her coffee. "My final thesis would have said as much. But I was too busy." She offered a thin-lipped smile. "Women today are so lucky. We can have it all." A wave of a hand, a clarification. "Just not all at once."

She smoothed her trousers. "How important is a *final* thesis anyway?" She'd already written papers for all of her classes, she explained. "What was just one more?"

Instead, Regina had registered for several graduate courses in what she called the "exciting, new field of educational assessment" at an online university in Arizona—it's much more "intense," she said, "when you study at home"—and not long after, secured a management role with an organization advertising "data driven curriculum consultations" to universities nationwide. She got what she wanted. (Regina always got what she wanted.) Now, after her morning workout session and before her drive to the office, she spent her "idle time" (as she liked to call it) writing back-cover copy for a local publisher of romance novels, which naturally, she explained, she never read herself.

"Of course I don't read them," she liked to say. "There's romance, secrets, a big payoff." She laughed. "Only the details change."

Outside, the children screeched. We both ignored them. Regina directed my attention back to her catalog. This time to a "Proustian" tea set. "Check this out." She leaned intently over her mug. At once, her chin looked moist.

I tried to mimic the offhand sincerity of her voice—"Wow," I offered—and I was rewarded at once with a small smile before some exploit outside (a big stick was involved) caught her eye again.

"We really should be off." She kept it short and sweet, shook my hand, and promised to drop off a few more catalogs the next time she was out walking the dog. A moment later, she made a beeline for what the community pamphlet called her Neo-Queen-Anne-Colonial-with-Tudor-Highlights built at six o'clock on the circle.

Jimmy trailed after her in a pair of mud-encased sneakers.

He grinned as Bobby waved goodbye.

I was pleased until I realized my son's "wave" had ended with a subtle chop to the neck.

A mother is always betrayed.

CHAPTER NINE

Gild the Lily

From that day on, Regina dropped home improvement catalogs through our mail slot every morning without fail. After Ed's remoteness—his almost complete seclusion in his study—her attentions at first were welcome. They soon wore thin, as the predictable smack of bound glossy pages onto our wood floor each day became as common a sound in our house as our aged boiler's drunk-uncle sputter and flare when it grumbled to life with the dawn.

At first I figured she was still uneasy about Jimmy's behavior, that the catalogs were a surrogate for a foreseeable future apology. But remorse wasn't Regina's style. The truth, I soon realized, was that Regina was cleaning house. The catalogs took up too much space in her perfect, dust-free Hummer home: she preferred they clutter my slope-floored farmhouse instead. In no time at all, my old closet was stuffed with her remorseless gifts, a towering toner-cured stack that choked up our small space with astonishing speed. I couldn't even dump the magazines until she left town. At the time, it seemed crass. I didn't want to offend.

So, like a chump, I held onto Regina's trash. While she, in turn, stole my marriage. How could I have known Ed was often upending my neighbor behind the faux ficus in her back parlor. That he was—as my son's adolescent pals might have said—in a bush. In the bush.

Bobby, of course, would never have said that to me. But what he might have discovered about Ed and Regina? To my shame I'll now never know.

I have my suspicions. One Saturday afternoon, I let myself fall into a midday nap with the baby after watching dust motes waltz above me in the streaming light. I awoke to a much less peaceful feeling: there was weight to the air. Mass. The dust had collected around me into a murder of crows. A murmuration.

The realization arrived suddenly as I moved from one world to another.

Smoke.

Grabbing the baby, I followed my nose down the hall to the foyer. There, Bobby stood in the doorway. In front of him, the closet that Regina's garbage occupied was open. The stacked magazines tilted to one side, the peak already avalanched onto the floor. I at once saw that he was transfixed: the magazines were smoldering, their exposed edges black and curling into a dense gassy sweat, while others were fully alight like candles on the limbs of a tree.

"Bobby!"

He jumped when I touched his shoulder. And—did I imagine it?—the edge of a matchbook winked from his pocket. In the flickering light, he looked pale.

There was no time to look closely. No time to ask. Instead, I shouted for Ed, pulled the children out the back door to safety. By the time I returned with our small kitchen fire extinguisher, it had little effect.

A few minutes later, a fire truck pulled up. And whatever was in Bobby's pocket was gone.

The fire chief speculated that, like corn in a silo, the physics of fermentation had lit up the tightly packed closet. Amplified by the farmhouse's dry wooden lathe—"kindling," he called it—my foyer was scorched in no time at all. No accelerant required.

"Like hay in a barn, you mean?" It was all I could muster as I stood out on the sidewalk, warm from the afterglow of my smoldering porch. Regina had taken the baby to her house. As usual, Ed was nowhere to be found.

The chief nodded. "Happens sometimes." He took his helmet off; and as he shuffled his feet, a sludge of charred magazine pages gently lapped over his boots onto my slippers.

I felt my face caving in—a black hole in my heart that began with Ed. And was beginning to swallow my son.

The chief saw only a confused woman. He put what was meant to be a comforting, Kevlar-coated arm around the parchment of my bare shoulders.

"I'll explain it at all to your husband," he said with kind condescension. "You go get some rest."

He must have already been accustomed to the caustic air around us because my bitter smile didn't faze him one bit.

Perhaps he really thought the fire made sense.

Perhaps he thought he'd even find Ed.

Good luck. I didn't say it out loud.

I also didn't tell him what I'd seen in my son's pocket—after all, I wasn't sure what I'd seen in my son's pocket—and as the chief walked away, gathering equipment along the sidewalk, barking orders at his men, he called Bobby over to the truck with a friendly wave and showed him how to crank the deflated hose back onto its wheel. In no time at all, Bobby was hard at work.

From the corner of my eye, I watched Bobby as he chatted the firemen up, kept them in stitches.

As though nothing strange had happened at all.

It didn't occur to me until much later that Bobby must have discovered that Regina had stolen his father. That her affability was nothing more than a ploy: she needed us the way a belly button needs the lint trapped inside its gummy, overheated cavity.

From Ed:

You mean she didn't need you at all.

Exactly.

How much easier for Bobby to be angry with me than with his father. Or his friend's mother. Is it so surprising? It's hard to feel fury for a neighbor you rarely see. Or a parent who no longer opens their door.

Even Regina admitted during the trial that she wasn't "against" me, so much as she was "for" Ed. Either way you parse the syntax of their affair, it was Regina who called the police to report Ed missing. She who led the police to believe I did him in because, as she testified a few months later, blinking her waxy, doe eyes at my hearing: "Jane was jealous of our love."

Maybe she's right. If I had known back then what was in store for my family, I surely would have lit Bobby's matches myself. But I would have struck them at her house. Even now, imagining her overstuffed goose-feathered sectional as the gas-soaked wick that set her home alight brings me more pleasure than I should admit.

Ed and Regina tag-teamed me, that's the truth. My husband set me up for the fall. Then my neighbor put me away.

My one consolation? Regina now thinks Ed is dead. And all she has left is poor, dull Bernard for an ex-husband. Not to mention a stooge of a son who still roughs kids up.

Celeste scribbles in the margins something about Regina's glutes that I should not transcribe—though, in the interest of truth, "flat-assed whore" isn't accurate. Sure, Regina's avocados are often enhanced by expertly tailored linen slacks. But I've been to pool parties with her, seen the evidence strapped into place by the cheeky architecture of a Lycra-lined swimsuit. I remain determined, however, to take the high road. My children must know that even under duress my values hold firm. If I can't be with them, perhaps one day—when they read this book—they'll at least know I held steady. That I stayed true. That, above all else, I remain worthy of their respect.

This memoir is all I have to convey the depth of my love.

"*Respect?*" I imagine #3 rolling his eyes. He's the quiet one who only speaks when he has something cruel to say. Evidently, his mother failed to pass on one of life's essential lessons.

I do not dignify him with a response.

"Good show," Celeste whispers and pats my hand. The gesture, I gather, is meant to be reassuring, but I feel like the last man at the gate as the hordes rush in.

What could I have said to Regina to set her off? She was so insistent at my commitment hearing that I hated Ed. But—really—who *hasn't* moaned, at one time or another, that she "could just kill" her spouse for (insert X grievance here), especially after several glasses of a tawny port (my preferred vintage) during the night's darkest hours, when the kids are in bed, your friends are few, and your husband is working late—again—in his study.

All to say: Regina didn't have to try hard to get me drunk. But even soused, I didn't mean what I said to her. Of *course* I didn't mean all the things I said, all the times I said them. For a supposed student of literature, Regina has a tin ear. And now my protestations fall on the Board's deaf ones.

"Did you want to be caught?" BM3 intones. "Why else

would you admit your fiendish plans" (yes, he said "fiendish") "to a neighbor with whom you had" (a pause here) "a *history?*"

I remind them, as I often remind them, that I had no history with Regina *then*. That my so-called "history" with her began later, in the future of that long past present. And that, just like them, I learned the day of the hearing that she and Bernard had separated. Even if I had discovered by then that she'd been sleeping with Ed.

Yet the Board's insinuation has some merit: it was I who let the cat into the birdcage when the bird's wings had been clipped.

Even now, they won't let the point go.

From Ed:

You never let things go either.

"Why," BM2 asks time and again, "would you exaggerate your feelings to a 'confidant' when the truth," he goes on with seeming innocence, "stands in well enough for itself?"

It must be a trick question.

"Really," I say, "who *wouldn't* gild a story with such a captive audience? Lipstick doesn't change a smile, does it? It just tints your lips a more pleasing shade of pink.

"All good stories, even one as odd as mine," I go on, "have a bit of play to them." I try to smile. "Every story does."

It's the most I've spoken since I arrived. Celeste doesn't look happy. And BM4 is suddenly looking at me attentively over his beaten doorknob of a nose.

"Do you think you're a writer like your brother Jules, then?"

His pencil drums the table thoughtfully and, across the room, Celeste's eyes widen in alarm. She doesn't need to say a word. This counter-memoir is a secret between us. Not only is my manuscript "none of their business," she says, but she's worked "damn hard" to prevent my long-concealed role at my brother Jules's side from rising into public discussion.

"We must be careful," she's counseled. "Your family history

of authorship and unusual endings," as she likes to call them, "could be prejudicial," particularly with respect to (she fears) "your brother's much mythologized death."

It's true. Jules's inexplicable end—in my childhood bed no less—remains the source of countless conspiracy theories.

But if two men I'd loved had both "experienced misadventure" (as she calls it) while writing books about my odd family?

"That's two men," Celeste says, "too many."

"Let's just," she advises, "steer clear of creating any undue suspicion."

It's a delicate path she's carved for me. So I am exceptionally mindful of what I say back to BM4.

"A writer? Have you ever read a book with my name on it?"

My tone is a tad too prim—I feel like a hooker in a highnecked collar—but I'm lucky. BM4 rocks back in his chair, the idea that had begun to simmer at the base of his skull at once going flat without any added heat from me. He's not so hard to read. Bored, his thoughts turn elsewhere: no doubt, there's a three-day weekend on the horizon for the liberated. I imagine #4 renting a cabin, stocking it with a tired wife, two television-starved kids and a gassy, overweight dog. I can read his face: the wrinkled lemur thinks he might get lucky. There's a mild flush to his skin as he slides his pencil behind his ear.

It never crosses #4's mind to ask me about Jules's books. He never considers that I played any role in their production. My mother's talent at orchestrating our familial deception remains, even now, invisible to outsiders: Jules, they think, was a teen prodigy. A publishing marvel. I, just a quiet but supportive college-aged sister. To them, it still seems my mother nurtured us both. They see what she wanted them to see.

Someone like you, she'd often intone, *is the architect, the trace that holds ideas together. You are the spine. Not the voice.* Then she'd give me that look, the one she knew I couldn't deny when I was on the verge of giving up. *Jules loves you,* she'd say. *He needs you.* Touching my shoulder. We all *need you.*

What she meant: Bite your tongue. Don't be a brat. Don't muck up the family meal ticket.

There's no defense from a mother's language when it's tethered to a lash.

Then, one day, without warning, Jules OD'd on painkillers. In my bed. Waiting for me to come home.

I don't think I've ever recovered.

Ghostwriter. Housewife. Mother. I've been trained to silence myself in countless ways. How many libraries are filled with books that bear men's names, but were written by the women who cooked their meals? Bore their children? Brought them Cheetos or Cola slushies from the corner store when they asked?

How can we ever know?

Later, Celeste congratulates me on what she calls my "precise diction." Delving into "old controversies," she reflects, would have been "unwise."

I choke. "Did I have a choice?" I ask her, the heat rising under my scalp. Each follicle quivers; the waxy derm layer wrapping my skull seems to melt. I am a candle. In a moment my head will light up. Can't she see?

My hands clench the arms of my chair. It's awfully hard to breathe.

She arches one eyebrow. "Let's just steer clear of," she pauses, "*complications* surrounding Jules's books. Or his death."

She gives me a long look I can't read. "Don't you think that's best?"

"It will come up," I say. "You'll see. It always comes up. My mother will be the one to bring it up." There's bile in my throat. "She'll make me look damaged."

The word I don't use: *guilty.*

From somewhere nearby, an odd sound I can't place. It's Ed clapping, I realize.

Celeste waves a hand in dismissal. "Your mother will be focused on her custodial application." Her tone is all business. "If she wants to be named your children's guardian, she'll keep her ideas about Jules to herself. She needs to seem sweet and steady."

She touches my shoulder gently. My mother never touched my shoulder gently.

"Write it down *here*," she advises, tapping the pages fanned out on the table. "Keep quiet in *there*." She gestures toward the room where I meet with the Board. Then leans back, waits. My answer is important to her. It's a test.

When I at last nod, Celeste's relief is palpable. We are on the same page.

As I have a thousand times before, I let Jules go because I must. Because there is nothing else I can do. Because my brother is dead. And I could not save him. Or myself. Because proving my past won't alter my present. Jules's books? My role in writing them? That story won't unlock BPI's doors. Or return my life to its proper shape. It won't bring back my kids.

Outside the small window I cannot reach, there is only sky, a passing wisp of cloud. An occasional intemperate bird stutters past. Then the shadow of a butterfly. A leaf.

Celeste takes my hand: she has become very good at reading my mind.

"One day, your children will see your work."

She taps the manuscript I've been working on.

"*Your* work. That's what this book is for."

She says it gently, to remind me, as if I could have forgotten, that I'm compiling this account for my son and daughter. That this counter-memoir—unlike my husband's or my brother's books—is wholly my own creation.

These pages are corrective.

I'm finally adding my own words to the story. Taking great care to sort truth from lies.

"You're being circumspect," Celeste notes approvingly.

I nod, pleased that she sees my point, until much later that evening when, fuzzy from the pills the nurse brings before the lights dim, I'm reminded of something Ed once said. That he's right now whispering into my ear:

Without lies, there's no truth at all.

Here I pause, as I will often pause in the pages to come, to take note of my bearings when they go off course:

Ed, leave my memoir to me, I think (I write). Don't interfere. Let me have these words. This page.

As for you, I admonish myself, stick to the facts. Be direct. Don't quibble. Embellish. That's exactly what Ed wants.

Keep the lines precise between fact and fiction.

Tell this story straight.

MEMOIR

"Once upon a time they began it is begun."

"We go back to the apartment. We are lovers. We can't stop loving each other."

"She is here. I will be fine. The air is rich with her exhalations."

"It is commonly known that those nearest to us, those of whom we have the most extensive, intimate knowledge, are often held at arm's length in our minds. The saying rolls so easily off the tongue: 'familiarity breeds contempt,' and the idiom 'to take for granted' is as familiar to us as those we do."

"Could it be that he was in love with her, then, remembering the misery, the torture, the extraordinary passion of those days?"

"What creature was it, that, masked in an ordinary woman's face and shape, uttered the voice, now of a mocking demon, and anon of a carrion-seeking bird of prey?"

"Sometimes one meets a woman who is beast turning human."

"He had grabbed her and was holding her entirely in his fist."

"The others relay her story. She is married to her husband who is unfaithful to her. No reason is given. No reason is necessary except that he is a man."

COUNTER-MEMOIR

"Collaborators, we smile at each other our honest smiles."

"I remember how, that night, I lay awake in the wagon—lit in a tender, delicious ecstasy of excitement, my burning cheek pressed against the impeccable linen of the pillow and the pounding of my heart mimicking that of the great pistons ceaselessly thrusting the train that bore me through the night, away from Paris, away from girlhood, away from the white, enclosed quietude of my mother's apartment, into the unguessable country of marriage."

"Reader, I married him."

"I closed the study door softly behind me, stood in the hall, and counted to a thousand. Then stamped up to the guest-room, where I swept the cobwebs off the ceiling as though I were pulling hair and completely wrecked what little nail polish I had opening the side guest-room window so I could shake the mop out over the open study window just below. I scrubbed the bathroom floor and cleaned out the closet and washed down the hall woodwork and then I took a shower and came downstairs, and made dinner, and I was feeling very righteous and forgiving until my husband glanced down at his chicken cutlet and asked absently if he had remembered to tell me that I was a marvelous cook."

"In a way, her strangeness, her naïveté, her craving for the other half of her equation was the consequence of an idle imagination."

"It was then that she experienced the faint awareness of his potential for meanness."

"You want to see all of a woman, as much as possible. You don't see that for you it's impossible."

"I am broken like a nut between two rocks, granite and granite."

"I stood there, there in the sunlight, and thought that I didn't as yet know what I wanted. I now fully knew what I didn't want and what and whom I hated. That was something."

CHAPTER TEN

The Invisible Nib

The thick institutional furniture at Buffalo Psychiatric juts out at inconvenient angles. My shins are bruised, the backs of my thighs puckered a cantankerous yellow. But each bump and thud as I wander the halls reminds me that I'm alive, that—no matter the medications the nurses deliver in their harmless paper cups with uncanny regularity—I'm nowhere as numb as they'd like me to be. Sure, my hips ache from (the now) inevitable fender benders with sturdy armchairs stained by weepy warts, rheumy eyes, and needle jacks. But each bruise, I'm determined to think, is a sign of hope. I *feel*. Even now—against all odds—I still can *feel*.

The present tense gives me power over my alien past.

That's what I tell myself, at least. What I hold to when, over breakfasts of lukewarm hash, I long for the baby's breath on my cheek. Bobby's wiry arm hooked inside mine as we walk.

But the past is tricky. It pushes the present around like a bully. There's no recourse or remedy. Look at me. I've tried calling for help. It hasn't done any good at all.

No one believes me.

Why would anyone believe a wife who claims that, one day, her husband went to his study to work on a book, and that he, simply, never came out?

I often imagine I'm a swimmer struggling against a rough current. On good days I convince myself that, if I just angle in slowly toward land, I've got a shot at the shoreline. But the alternative weighs me down. In Buffalo, you hear stories all the time. Some tourist dips a toe into the river. Then, in a flash, loses his footing and gets sucked out by the Niagara's hypnotic force into the hydroelectric turbines downstream. By the time rescuers find him—*if* they find him—on the other side of the falls, what's left has been broken by steel and rock alike. Maybe the trout will call his ribcage home. But most often, the body will just disappear.

Here, Celeste's pen has left a dent in the paper where its dry nib once pressed into the page. It's not hard to imagine her pausing, hunched pensively at her desk, a cup of coffee cooling at her side, as she suddenly considered posing me a direct question that her advanced legal training has taught her not to ask.

Evidently, this page offers the atmosphere of a secret confession. As if my imagined tourist's fate were Ed's.

But see the clean margins? Celeste hasn't asked. She'll never ask if I killed Ed. If I'm the reason he disappeared. She's not supposed to. Doesn't want to.

Still, she's left a mark for me here, a negative impression on this page that, like a shoe print by an open window, suggests I ought to take more care.

It's hard not to see her "point."

So let me be clear for the record:

No, Celeste. Ed did not drown. Not as far as I know.

My missing husband, who was raised in a small town by the sea that no longer exists, avoided the water. When his phobia began—whether it was before or after his Illyrian village was driven into the sea by their border neighbors—he never told me. I can only say that, in all the years we lived in Buffalo, Ed never hiked the mild paths that weave along Lake Erie's shores. Or strolled the rocky trails above the Niagara's teeming waters. As for the falls? He never walked the famed promenade on the Canadian side. Or hiked around the park at Goat Island on ours. Even at the inevitable pool parties thrown by our neighbors, he kept his distance. He was the guy who always stood by the grill. The reliable hand that refilled the cooler. The friend who could be counted on to chat up a recent sunburn victim deep in the bowels of a home—far from the water's edge.

The running neighborhood theory was that vanity drove Ed's behavior. My husband still had an impressive mop of hair at his age; and whether he was heading to the office, or mowing the lawn, he always primped before going public. The balding husbands nearby admired him for it. And hated him for it. But the truth was harder to explain. Quite simply, Ed didn't trust me or our (so-called) friends near the water, and there was no good way to explain his phobia without dredging up all manner of atrocities. The gristled remains of the short, televised modern war that first drove his family from their home, then their country completely, were subjects much too sensitive for our neighbors' carefree ears as we strolled around their hardscaped backyards or drank their dirty martinis. Even I didn't know the extent of his trauma until we moved to the farmhouse and the inground pools all around us became a regular feature of our lives. It is one thing to fear the uncharted depths far from home. Quite another, the chlorinated waters of a four-meter lap pool. How could I have known?

One evening, shortly before our first barbecue, he called me into the kitchen, sat me down at the table, and admitted that, after ten years of marriage, he still didn't trust me—not one bit. Not around the water.

While he talked, he was coring an apple. Pulling its hard center out. While leaving the flesh of the fruit intact.

"One day," he said casually, "you'll push me in."

I protested.

What kind of thing was that to say to his wife? To the mother of his then nine-year-old son?

He shrugged. "You'll have a good reason. Maybe you'll think giving me a nudge will help me. Give me character. Just like we sometimes push our boy."

I was dumbfounded.

"That's crazy, Ed."

I tried to stay calm. But he was—suddenly—a strange creature. Someone I didn't know. He looked like the Edward G. Tamlin I'd married. But this Ed had musky, edged shoulders, a much harder chin. Where had he been hiding?

He didn't blink. "Is it?" Then he shrugged. "Why give fate another shot?"

Any spouse can imagine my deep confusion. Yet as he began his precise work on the core of a new apple, another emotion slowly rose up and took its place. Inexplicably, I began to feel honored that Ed "trusted" me enough to admit he didn't trust me at all, even pride in his failure—the flaw he'd been willing to share—because he'd chosen to share it with *me*. Ed still wanted me in his life, even though he seemed to believe there was a very real chance that one day I might kill him.

Before me, my Board-appointed therapist is rapt. Her name, I've been told, is Madeleine, though most everyone calls her Dr. M. Her hair is blond and looks as crisp as a dried copse of cuttleweed. The urge to touch it is hard to resist.

"Ed was experiencing what we call a 'second-strike phenomenon,'" she explains, hands fluttering between us. "It's not unusual for survivors of violence to develop obstructive behaviors that inhibit, even preclude, emotional and physical intimacy."

Now she's curious. "Second-strike patterns tend to get worse with age." She pauses. "Were they a nuisance to your marriage?"

She asks the question so sweetly, I'm nearly disarmed. But I pinch myself—hard—no doubt adding yet another blemish to the artwork on my left thigh.

"We had some troubles," I nod.

With a small frown, she jots something in her pad.

"Ed was sincere," I elaborate quickly. "So it took me longer than it should have to realize he was more than just," I search for the right word, "*distant*. In a store, on a plane, he always knew where the exits were. I should have known that, one day, he'd look for a way out of our marriage too."

It's the nature of her occupation that gloomy disclosures make her happy. A soothing, birdlike sound warbles in the back of her throat as she sighs and sits back. Then, just as I think it's time to go—as I begin to gather my paper-thin housecoat and rise from my chair—she shoots off a final question, as though it's suddenly just occurred to her.

"Was Ed a good father?"

I wobble, and she knows she's caught me off guard. Just as she intended.

"Of course," I say firmly, straightening my back. "Ed loved his children."

My tone isn't defensive. But my qualifier undermines all my hard work. Every "of course," "I'm sure," and "no doubt," she's told me, "augments uncertainty" (her words) rather than diminishing it. The more convinced I seem, the more skeptical she becomes. And she doesn't hide it.

"Certainty breeds blindness," she once explained, failing to note the patent irony of her own conviction. I suppose I should have said something. But it wasn't wise to correct my caseworker, I decided. I could imagine her notes about my condition changing, and my "amnesia"—what she called a "neuroleptic interruption"—suddenly rediagnosed as a "pathology of deceit." That was the Board's preferred option. She had told me. More than once.

"That's what they think," Madeleine said at the end of our first meeting. "But I'm on your side, you have to believe me." She stared at me hard. "Trust me, trust the process." Melting into a smile. "We'll get through this together."

But we weren't together. The process had trapped me in this godforsaken place. And her analytical skills seemed at best uneven. It was evident—at the very least—that she didn't turn her maxims on herself.

So I let the remark pass. Why tempt fate? I'd learned at least that much from Ed.

"So I should be tentative? Uncertain?" I asked.

She leaned forward, her eyes firm and gray, for the first time unreadable.

"When you know the answer to that question," she said, "we'll be ready to part ways."

Now her broad smile—oversaturated with unearned friendship—suggests we're nowhere near that final phase in my treatment. But I'm lucky: she doesn't pursue it. And when the orderly raps twice, she waves me out the door.

The Board, on the contrary, won't let the issue rest.

"Was your husband right?" BM2 has red ears. His jowls quiver with excitement.

It's not the first time I wonder what his wife must be like. How did he come to believe a husband could be "right" without any qualification at all?

"Right?" I repeat. I'm confused.

"That you'd kill him one day."

Leave it to the Board to take a story about trust and turn it inside out.

"I did not kill Ed."

I say it slowly, giving weight to each word, anchoring the sentence (I hope) in the shallow marina of the Board's collective imaginations.

Unfortunately, the stress makes my eczema flare—my elbows start to itch, then my ear, the back of my neck—and I'm sure I suddenly look like a restless, unnerved animal. They have no idea how difficult it is for me not to stretch and have a go at the inflamed patch on my left hip. How hard it is for me to remain still. When everything in my nature resists.

We stare at each other, BM2 and I, like parents fighting when their children are within earshot. Then our time is up, the session breaks, and, out in the hall once again, an orderly at my side, I give in completely. By the time I arrive at my room, my fingernails are wet with shredded skin and blood.

The orderly doesn't say a word. He just hands me ointment, a bandage. Then he's gone down the hall, the rubber soles of his orthopedic shoes squeaking softly on the overwaxed linoleum.

It's the first and last sound I hear each day.

As usual, the Board, like my therapist, is onto something.

Just not the right thing.

Or, more precisely, the right thing. But from the wrong point of view.

The truth isn't relative: anyone who's ever found themselves on the wrong side of a locked jail cell can tell you that. Like looking through a pair of 3D glasses, it's only when you position the frames on your nose precisely that the truth jumps out, touches you with its uncanny dimensionality.

Suddenly, what is flat becomes round. There's always more to know.

The problem is that facts lurk in every corner, changing the register, the way the truth adds up. In the library here (filled with nonfiction because it's less "vexing" for the patients, I'm told) I nonchalantly page through a book on "defunct theories" during my Library Encounter Time. Who knew that Pythagoras—the Greek mathematician who designed a theorem every kid learns in geometry class— proved the earth was round as early as the sixth century B.C.? Yet it wasn't until Columbus sailed off to the New World a millennium later that the public came to believe it. Even now (I read), as satellites circle the earth, transmitting images of our planet's marbled suspension in space, advocates of "flat earth theory" continue to congregate, if in ever-whittling flocks.

Yet I'm the one who's been locked up.

My L.E.T. complete, I scratch an elbow back in my room, climb into bed. Hold my breath while I roll my face into the pillow. I'm a swimmer, I decide. One that Ed can't touch. How long can I hold my breath in my oxygen-deprived environment before I have to rise again and fill my lungs with Lysol-scented air?

On my first go: eighty-three seconds.

Not bad. But next time, I'll do better. Next time, I'll come up with more concrete answers to my therapist's questions. I'm in training, now. I have to prepare for the unpredictable. Stay sharp.

Madeleine's question wasn't specific enough. It missed the point. Was Ed a good father? Of course he was. But was Ed a good father to *both* of our children? Was he the *same* father to our daughter as he'd been to our son?

Second-strike phenomenon, she called it.

I'll say.

Everyone wants to know my secret: they want to know what happened to Ed.

But that's a mystery. Not a secret.

The only real secret I've kept since my family's demise is the one I've kept from my daughter. Not from shame. Or fear.

But to protect her. To keep my baby from knowing one day what she must in fact one day know.

Make the prick quickly, Celeste advises.

In the background, Ed mutters words I cannot repeat. But he cannot stop me now.

It is with regret, my darling girl, that I write this.

Your father, Edward Tamlin, never acknowledged your birth. By "acknowledge" I mean he did not hold you. He did not feed you or change you. He did not once rock you.

He wasn't even there the day you were born.

I have scratched out these words countless times. Countless times I've added them back.

Damned if I do.

Even now, I wonder if my girl should learn of the cloud around her first months of life. I know what it's like to survive a father's rejection. To feel as though you weren't enough to keep the first man in your life close to your heart. A small cavity erodes inside your skull and, over time, it fills with a corrosive gas that makes you lightheaded as it slowly eats away at your thoughts.

I'd save my baby that pain. But Celeste—wise Celeste—has convinced me otherwise.

"We all have baggage," she says matter-of-factly. "You can't protect your girl from her history. A missing father. An imprisoned mother. That's," she searches for a tactful description, "an unavoidable turn of events."

She clears her throat. "Better for *her*"—she stresses this last pronoun and at once wins me over—"that she knows you stood by her, that you were her advocate, her protector, from day one. That, though her life began with injustice, you strove to amend her injuries with a mother's love and care."

Celeste's hands are lightly clenched, and I wonder, suddenly, about her own father. But before I can ask, she goes on, and my mild question about her parent continues to be (by this most recent draft) ignored.

"That's hope, don't you see?" she says. "Even if it's lined with sadness. Your gift to your daughter should be *hope*. Not lies."

Perhaps we all learn from our fathers too well.

CHAPTER ELEVEN

Sleeping Dogs Lie

From the moment I told Ed we had a second child on the way, he began to look ghostly. Slightly out of phase. I didn't think much of it at first. Ed was still working at his law firm then, and, like any other dad, he left in the morning smelling like soap, and returned home at night in a fog of stale air and spent coffee. After he took off his suit, he'd hunker down at the kitchen table and, if he was in a good mood, let Bobby regale him with the humdrum harmonics of the day's events. On weekends, it was more of the same: on Saturday mornings, he'd wave to our neighbors as he mowed the lawn. An hour later, he'd retreat into the den to watch a game with our son, and they'd often both just fall asleep on the couch. It was easy to think Ed just seemed distracted. After all, he often was.

It was a good life. For some dull. But for Ed and me—who'd had childhoods filled with upheaval—stability was an immense, even an incalculable, pleasure. That's what he said. That's why we moved to the suburbs. And if I sometimes complained that we could no longer walk to an art gallery or a café as we had in the city, Ed would glance at our son, remind me how well Bobby was doing. *This* home wasn't our last home. Just be patient, he'd say.

"Look to the long term." Those were his words. So I stuck to them, kept to our plan.

That Ed made the plan, and then—without telling me—stepped off its path, is the kind of irony I steer clear of now. It does me no good at all.

From my therapist: something like applause . . . though it only reaches her eyes. Her training, I've discovered, bars her from more physical displays of approval.

In a strange way, this silent exchange with her embodies the full range of emotional interplay characterizing my entire life.

Shortly after I revealed I was pregnant, a subtle hitch crept into my conversations with Ed—a delay, as though we were on opposite ends of a bad phone connection. He'd pause while he took in the simple fact of my words, the way they vibrated the air. Then stare at me as if I didn't make sense. He often apologized for it. Gave me a bemused (even endearing) smile when he realized what he'd done (again). I'd get a quick hug or peck on the cheek. Occasionally, a grope: a quick hand up the shirt, a light slap on the bum. But then, without answering what I'd asked, he'd climb the stairs back to his office—and we wouldn't see him again for the rest of the night.

At first it was mildly amusing. Soon, it became annoying. Then, when I realized I'd stopped asking Ed questions completely—that I'd written him off—I knew trouble was on the horizon, the kind you don't just course-correct overnight. But I didn't know what to do.

I sometimes think that if I'd noticed his behavior sooner, I could have prevented him from slipping away completely. But I was preoccupied (understandably) by my pregnancy: my ballooning chest, my sodden ankles. Sure, my skin glowed.

I looked five years younger. But my ears rang, my thumbs twitched. And as soon as the baby was born, I knew I'd lose my temporary, deceptive revitalization. A candle burns brightest. Just before it burns out. For all that, I wasn't moody. Just uneasy. Like a dog howling right before an earthquake strikes, I sensed turmoil was on the horizon. Naturally, I thought my fears were tied to the baby. I didn't realize the coming seismic shift wasn't her impending arrival, but the unsteady ground already underfoot: a sinkhole swallowing Ed and me into the fathomless void of its abyss.

At the time, Ed's peculiar behavior seemed a natural, if undesirable, readjustment to our family's changing shape as we each, in our different ways, began to quarantine our private space before the new baby arrived. Even Bobby wasn't immune: one evening, I discovered him hoarding prized belongings (a small boat, a wooden peg, a plastic soldier he'd found in the street) behind a heating vent in his bedroom. Before he started pulling the floorboards up, I gave him a trunk with a key as a present, and promised him that we wouldn't open it unless he gave us permission. When I last saw him, my son was still wearing the key around his neck. Though the trunk itself had burned in the fire.

We never intended to have two children. That was the heart of the issue. As Ed put it, we needed "to be able to travel light." In his experience, only small families survived when catastrophe struck because they could make it on the run. An arithmetic for atrocity: one parent strapped a tot to their back; the other carried a gun. He refused to describe what had happened to his neighbors with two children or more. His lips would move. They might even begin to shape words in the language of his youth that he barely remembered. But, like a rag blown against a fence by a stiff wind, they'd get tangled up against his voice box, behind his teeth.

He'd choke.

So I wasn't mystified when Ed met the news of our daughter's arrival with trepidation. Yet Ed never asked me to end the pregnancy. (You should know that, my girl.) I never felt uneasy while he walked behind me down the basement stairs. And when, one evening, I tripped hard after he suddenly stretched his legs as he slept on the sofa, it was clearly my fault. The glass cocktail table broke under my awkward spill. But Ed was tender. Almost mournful as he patched a cut on my arm.

I considered driving to my obstetrician's office that night for a checkup. Instead, I stayed home, sat on the couch, and held Ed's hand to comfort him while my belly cramped. Sure, my hip ached when I woke the next morning, but I knew I'd made the right decision. By the time the eleven o'clock news flashed across the screen that night, Ed looked less grave. Even at peace.

In retrospect, I now know he'd made a decision.

One that changed all our lives.

For the worse.

One week later, Ed sat me down. It was a mild spring afternoon and we were lounging on the patio while Bobby played in the dirt nearby. Ed was in a good mood. He poured lemonade into our glasses and the ice clinked mildly as we sat back, looked into the sun together. His hand was on my thigh. When Bobby strayed off, it wandered up into the well of my lap.

When Ed began to explain, almost offhandedly, that he wanted to write a book—a "memoir" he called it from the start—I barely listened. His hand was busy at some mild work (I'll just say I was "preoccupied") and, to be frank, Ed often aired impulsive ideas. He was drawn to exotic cookbooks (which he quickly shelved). He signed up for countless "free first lessons" (fencing, yoga, French). And he was a regular purveyor of trendy home improvement kits, which quickly collected dust in our garage. His latest ambition, I thought, would garner the same commitment. So I did what most wives do. I closed my eyes. Smiled. Went along with his plan. Meanwhile, I began plotting how we might get Bobby to nap so we could work in some playtime ourselves.

I was certain Ed would forget his plan for a book as soon as he wrote the first page.

Madeleine raises an eyebrow at that.

"Certainty breeds blindness," I quickly intone.

She's downright pleased. Evidently, I'm making progress.

There were clues that his latest ambition was different—foremost, his specificity. As Ed explained, he wanted to document his mother's life. His father's betrayal. He wanted to write a story about his childhood home—a place that now existed only in his imagination—since there was nothing of his home, his village, or his country left. There ought to be a record about its disappearance, he said.

How could I disagree?

"Can a child's world vanish overnight?" he asked, watching Bobby heap gravel into the back of his toy truck. "If no one writes about the hamlet where I was born, who's to say it ever existed at all? That my family, our friends, mattered?" When he shifted on the lounge chair, my reflection jostled in the sunglasses hiding his eyes.

I rubbed my growing belly—our daughter wasn't due for another six months, but I had begun to thicken out, lose the severe cut of my cheekbones. I felt awkward, clumsy, irrepressibly horny—and my words took an equally imbalanced shape. Humor might have diffused his plan. Instead, I was much too direct.

My words, I now suspect, cemented his plans in place. Language is the crucible upon which my marriage—my life—has always foundered.

I reminded Ed that he had a new family, the young boy clattering just out of reach. He had *our* friends. *Our* colleagues. *Our* lives together.

Even Charlie Parker—licking her loins in a patch of sun, one long leg stretched behind her ear—relied on him. Bobby and I always forgot to feed her.

"You've made a new home for yourself." I waved my hand. "A new home *here*."

He sighed. "That's precisely my point: what if this world disappears too?"

He looked out over our mossy lawn, beyond the asphalt-tiled roofs of the homes surrounding our farmhouse, and off toward the horizon beyond them. A crescent of moon was in the sky at midday. A plane flew overhead.

I smiled, stroked his arm gently.

"That would never happen."

Yes, I once said that. Now knock on wood—on whatever terra firma is around you—and pray your world remains intact.

Two weeks later, Ed took a leave from his law firm.

His colleagues expected him back in six months, he said. Then he locked himself inside his den.

Eight months later I was selling our things—an old camera, a laptop, potted plants by our door, Ed's collection of baseball cards—to pay off the tax bill he had ignored. I told the neighbors who came to our door that we were scaling back, preparing for our "imminent move."

A simple lie, the kind you can turn out with a shrug and a laugh. But words have an incalculable power. They always come true. Though often not in the way you expect.

A year later, my children were taken. I was locked up here.

Not the "imminent move" I had imagined.

As for Ed? I never saw him again.

CHAPTER TWELVE

A Rose by Any Other Name

The baby's arrival was, like my pregnancy, slow and steady. Mild contractions began. I sent Bobby to Jimmy's house for the night and, an hour later, checked into the hospital. My husband was out of town, I told the nurses. I was alone. They shrugged: it was unfortunate, but they'd seen it before. They gave me a gown, reviewed my stats, and sent me off to walk the halls of the maternity ward. Not long after, my water broke. Five hours later—just as the witching hour clapped its hands in prayer—our girl was born, her eyes open, astonished, as the yellow fluorescent lights warmed her damp, shriveled skin. Covered in a fine white paste, she flexed her bony legs. Her mouth stretched: she mewled.

It's not difficult to have a baby on your own, I discovered. The same way it's not difficult to change a tire. Or clean the seasons from a gutter. It's not easy. There's plenty of sweat involved. Mistakes happen. You get banged up. Bruised. It would be nice to have someone to hold your hand, pass you a wrench. But, with a doctor at one end, a bedrail at the other, in time the job gets done.

Late the next day, I checked myself out. Infant in one arm, a small bag filled with diapers, a comb, ice packs, and pads, I waited alone in a wheelchair. When I was ready, I pretended to take a "call" from Ed on my cell.

His plane had just landed, I lied. The nurse had no reason to doubt me.

A few minutes later, a young volunteer wheeled me down to the lobby. "He'll be here shortly," I told her. She nodded, parked me in a warm spot near the window. With a gentle touch on the baby's arm, she was gone.

I was lucky, of course, that there were no complications. That the baby was in perfect health. Naturally, I was sore—the enormous pad in my crotch felt like a half-scaled trout as I hobbled out toward my car—but the baby soon tucked into her car seat didn't notice me wince. Nor had anyone else. My limp, my frown, didn't look at all out of place on a hospital sidewalk. I seemed mildly damaged. Just like every other patient nearby.

When I got home Ed was in his study where I'd left him—I heard his office chair creak as I passed outside in the hall—and, setting my girl in her bassinet by my bed, I collapsed at once and fell asleep. When I woke the next morning to the baby's unpracticed complaints—a chorus of mewls, snorts and grousing huffs—I fed her at once. Then called Regina to send Bobby home. She didn't ask where I'd been.

Bobby was a trooper. He helped make dinner that first week. Sandwiches. Or the microwaveable dinners I'd stocked up as my due date approached. For him, it was all a treat. He touched his sister's tiny fingers and toes with delight.

"She's not very pretty." He was worried about her as she contorted her face and huffed.

"All babies are ugly at first," I explained. "Just give her a few weeks. You'll see."

That was enough to reassure him.

As for Ed, he never held the baby. Never heard her cry out to be nursed.

He never even helped me pick out her name.

One day, she was Olivia, the next Susan. Soon after that Bethany. None of my careless names stuck. Though she often complained, it was not about us, her name(s), her brother's mild envy. She sensed she would soon enter our lives the way an actor walks onto a stage: she was just waiting for the right scene to step out from the curtain, to say her first lines, and begin her role in our drama.

Even now, I just call her Baby.

Choking Games

Erotic and autoerotic asphyxiation (EA and AEA, respectively) are acts of sexual strangulation performed on a lover or on oneself, which are designed to intensify orgasm by restricting oxygen to the brain. During EA and AEA, the carotid arteries are compressed, and the resultant hypoxia is said to amplify sexual pleasure.

EA and AEA are most often performed with ligatures such as ties, ropes, sheets, cords, or belts. Suffocation from placing a plastic bag over the head or inhaling gas or solvents is also common.

The practice of autoerotic asphyxia can be dangerous and results in a number of accidental deaths every year: 500 to 1,000 victims annually, according to one study.

EA and AEA should not be confused with a thrill-seeking behavior practiced by adolescents called "the choking game" (also known as "the fainting game" and, at one time, "the flat-liner," "the pass-out challenge," "the Hammond," and "space monkey"). Documented since the 1930s, "the choking game" creates a drug-free state of euphoria that claims the lives of young people every year. The data varies, but at least one study claims 1,400 children died from choking game variants between 2000 and 2015.

Famous Autoerotic and Erotic Asphyxial Deaths

Peter Anthony Motteux. English playwright and translator. Publisher of *The Gentleman's Journal*. Accidental strangulation by prostitutes. First documented case of EA. 1718.

Kichizo Ishida. Restaurateur. Murdered during EA. His severed penis and testicles were discovered in his lover's handbag. 1936.

Albert Dekker. Stage and screen actor. Found in his bathtub, gagged and handcuffed. The word *vagina* scrawled in red lipstick on his stomach. *Cocksucker* on his chest. 1968.

Stephen Milligan. British politician and conservative MP. Discovered tied to a chair. Plastic bag over head. Plum stuffed in mouth. 1994.

Michael Hutchence. Australian singer-songwriter. Lead singer of rock band INXS. Discovered nude, hanging by belt, at the Ritz-Carlton, Sydney. 1997.

Gary Aldridge. Reverend, Thorington Road Baptist Church. Discovered hogtied and wearing two diving suits, including both a face mask and a head mask. 2007.

David Carradine. Body found in hotel closet, Thailand. Rope tied around neck and genitals. 2009.

CHAPTER THIRTEEN

Peel Back the Choke

Ed and I were never one of those couples who, friends whisper, were doomed from the start. Even after all that has happened, I still recall our early years fondly. Sure, we had bad moments, there were indiscretions. But I was happy: that's the truth. Our life was simple, our obstacles few. Ed joined an exclusive practice of real estate law. Our small apartment was bright and smelled like vanilla. Soon, Bobby came. Not long after, we moved: Bobby started school, I landscaped the yard, and our family appeared to neighbors and colleagues alike to be as definite and as orderly as the slate stones that formed a circular path around the ivy-clad perimeter of our farm. Our pleasures were simple then: on Sundays, Ed waxed the car, perhaps I stewed apples. Then I'd wrap my arm around his soft middle and we'd walk with Bobby to the park. But then Ed grew thin and I became sallow. He quit his job. I gave up on the garden. Soon, we refinanced the farmhouse, and I sold the potted ferns outside our front door to a neighbor who at once set them by hers.

I was supportive of his memoir at first: let me say on my own behalf that I have always been a good wife, that I believed Ed deserved a chance to fill his life with the indiscreet traffic of ink and paper, even though I had a troubled history with the world of print. So I made him tea, left him small meals by his door. I did not weep as I dumped the garbage on Tuesdays or when I tarred the roof because the ceiling leaked. I left Ed alone, that was his right. And he thanked me: at first, I found pages, then chapters, by my coffee mug in the morning, after he'd worked in his office while I slept in our bed, dreaming of a starless blue night which (I believed then) wrapped us together in the same cool embrace even if we seemed far apart.

So I can't help but blame myself. I gave Ed permission to write about our lives in his memoir. I consented, even encouraged, him to reflect on how *his* singular *life* became *our* plural *lives*. How his family, fleeing a small seaside village that no longer exists, arrived in the States, resettled, began a new life. How, one day, he then met me. It was enough, at that time, that he trusted me. That he'd asked for my help. Ed and I were working together—I was his initial reader—and, for the first time in my life, my history with Jules didn't feel quite so bad, even seemed to make sense. My skills finally had purpose; my past, new meaning. I even imagined the future "Acknowledgments" section in Ed's memoir where my name would soon appear. That simple fact sent me over the moon.

Yet as the weeks of writing grew longer, deeper, Ed became fully lost in thought. He often wandered down for dinner, absentmindedly asked Bobby about his day, and, without waiting for a reply, drifted away back up to his office. Later, after Bobby was tucked into bed, I'd find him standing alone in the hall as if he could no longer bear the steep consequentiality of the rooms in which we had once often gathered. Bobby was a source of comfort in those days. He'd just treat Ed as if he were a boy, pushing his father around as he did his own friends, until Ed would stumble forward, shaking his head loose from the funk that had foundered him, like a wet dog thick with bracken and leaves heaving itself from a pond. I blame myself: I should have seen what was coming. I should have known the drafts Ed left me were a sign, not a gift—an epitaph, not an archive—of our life together. Hadn't I watched Jules go through the same motions not long before he died?

Instead of kicking in Ed's door, I jotted brief notes in the margins. Underlined his diction when it became strained. And over the course of just a few months—how quickly my marriage unraveled!—I suddenly became a soloist in my life's common parlance: I no longer shared the paper or my pot of tea; I went on long walks by myself; I finished crosswords without his help. As for our habitual, if routine, gropings while Bobby napped? I satisfied myself by other means. I could wait, I counseled myself, alone in the dark. Soon, Ed's changes would come full circle. It wouldn't be long before he turned again on his axis and there, patiently waiting for me in his new orbit, I'd rediscover the man I'd lost.

I was a fool. Of course I was a fool.

Change is an infinite arbiter of the present. There's no accounting for when it may pause to acknowledge its fleeting reflection. Ed simply never did.

It was a philosopher's lesson. Not one meant for a wife, a ghostwriter, a lonely mother. How could I have guessed "absence" isn't the inverse of "presence"? That Ed's withdrawal wouldn't prompt a future return, but ongoing shades of privation whose depths even now I still can't imagine—an absence of absence which (if I follow this logic) suggests an absence still greater, far more profound, so very much *worse*, looming out there on the horizon, a wickedness just steps ahead, always breaking at the far edge of my vision? Let's call it the absence of absence of absence.

In shorthand: hell.

There are precedents, if I'd bothered to read them. For Tantalus, the grapes were always just out of reach. For Sisyphus, the stone always rolled back downhill. My punishment is of a different order: the slow amputation of my extended body. Ed has pared me back, stripped me of all that I have. My home, my children, my freedom, my face. He's peeled me down to the choke, exposed the soft flesh beneath my protective leaves. All I now have are these words.

So I sit here waiting—a bug transfixed by the breeze of an incoming swatter that's winding up to smack me flat.

"Take control," my therapist counsels. "Begin at *your* beginning. Tell me your story." She pauses. "Not his story."

"Herstory?" I say.

Madeleine nods, makes a mark in her notepad. The sun ravishes the barred windows. Why can't we all feel its heat the same way?

"Mystory?"

She nods again and waits this time. She doesn't hear it. Perhaps I don't either. Perhaps it was Ed who planted it right then in my mind. He can be so darn cheeky.

Mystery?

All right then, my darling. Let's begin the descent.

It's only one letter away.

CHAPTER FOURTEEN

A Language of Limbs

If a story really begins when its characters become aware they have a story to tell—that they *are* the story the way a cloud is luminous rain—then "my story" (as my therapist still calls it against my will) begins one month after Bobby was injured. It starts the day my daughter—then just nine months old— became the subject of my husband's next "experiment."

Yes, Ed hurt my baby too.

Your own father made you into a rag doll, my darling. Stuffed you with old yarn and batting. Then he waited to see what would happen.

What kind of father hurts a baby? What kind of man breaks a mother, then watches as she tries to collect the scattered pieces of her life?

What kind of writer deploys the same plot twist twice?

The Board naturally doesn't see it that way. They focus on history, context. What they now call my "predisposition." On its own, Bobby's accident was just a dangerous fluke. But after the baby's "misfortune," they say a "pattern" rose into view.

I'd like to say that we simply diverge on the pattern's shape. But there's nothing simple about it.

The Board doesn't know my home. My family. They don't know my children's subtle shifts in temperament or behavior. How the baby puffed and grumped before gassing the nursery air. How Bobby's voice went pitchy if (when) he stole from the cookie jar I stored high on a shelf. I was—I *am* (see what they've taken from me?)—"the lady of the house." It is *my* home. I am responsible for the people in it. And in my home, I see what others do not. Like an optical illusion, I can see two faces staring, in conflict—while the Board only sees an innocuous vase. It's a matter of perspective: you must shift your whole worldview in order to even begin to imagine what it is that you've missed.

If they looked closely, they might see—instead of a "predisposition"—a woman who's been groomed, squeezed, into the well-defined contours of a familiar type. Ed isn't a womanizer. But I *was*, without a doubt, "woman-ized" by him. I don't know how he did it. I just know I'm not the wife and mother I tried to be. The kind of wife and mother I wanted to be. Instead, I've become someone only Ed would desire. A character without much character at all.

Too much chit chat. A note from Celeste. *Time to tell us what happened to the baby.*

Celeste's job is to keep me on course. In so many different ways.

First, let me give credit where credit is due. It was Bobby who rescued the baby. I didn't fail my children once. I failed them twice.

It was a Saturday. The early fall. Outside, the air was mild, cool, the leaves of the old oak tree beyond the kitchen window already glowing with inner iridescent life. Inside, it was much less peaceful. A college football game was playing in the den: hoots and whistles roared though the house; the aging plaster and lathe powdered up with each stereophonic bump and thud. Bobby was sprawled on the couch—his bum leg propped on a pillow—toying absently with the scab on his thigh as the baby played at his feet. It wasn't difficult to look after her as she banged blocks together, pulled shag from the carpet. If she drooled, there was no harm done. Occasionally, Bobby patted her head.

Naturally, I was in the kitchen. Like all mothers, I spend a good deal of time there. I also work in other rooms—make beds in bedrooms, rinse baths in bathrooms, launder in the laundry room—but, in Ed's mind, variation evidently resides only in the seasons or times of day.

This time, I wasn't making breakfast. I was cooking dinner. Meatloaf.

Bobby adores it, just like his father.

The baby? She won't eat it, even mashed with a spoon. Neither will I. But there I was, my hands deep in chopped beef and onion. We were all where we were supposed to be.

Bobby later told me that when he heard his sister mewling in her hungry kitten voice and turned to her, he at first believed she had gnawed on a red crayon she'd found under the couch. Or that she cut her lip when he wasn't looking. So when he saw her face smeared with streaks of red, he didn't panic. He did what any practical son of a practical mother would do: he pried open her mouth with his pinky and took a look inside.

That's when he saw the full extent of the problem.

"Mom?" he called.

Bobby's tone was familiar—concern and confusion inflected by mild adolescent urgency. He could have been calling for a midday snack. Chips. Sliced apples. String cheese.

Get a move on. Celeste's commentary is unusually cranky.

"Yes?"

I was distracted (I'll admit it) and though I tuned my antenna to his frequency at once, the football announcer's dull background banter was an oddly reassuring chaperone, so I kept kneading the clods of bright red beef, adding bread crumbs, an egg, diced tomato, a green pepper. A lump of meat fell onto my foot, sank between my toes: flesh, I noticed, that didn't really belong, but, flush against my skin, had already become as much "me" as a strand of the baby's hair stuck to the threads of my sweater.

"Mom?!" This time he shouted.

How could I have missed the fear in his voice?

There was a clatter. The baby howled.

I grabbed a towel and ran from the room.

CHAPTER FIFTEEN

Second-Strike Phenomenon

That's when this story changes.

That's when my whole world changed.

Back then, I didn't know lightning never strikes only once, let alone twice; in fact, lightning *always* strikes several times in rapid succession. The human eye just can't take it all in. That's what happened to the Diamond Beach boys—all three friends killed at one time by one bolt, or many bolts that looked like one—their feet charred in the same sandy spot where, not a moment before, they'd been playing.

One year later (almost to the day), lightning hit the beach again. One moment, twin sisters were building a castle. The next, the sand melted, transformed, and the girls were locked together inside a glass coffin.

In this story, there's no hope of a princely kiss.

Of course lightning never strikes twice. It strikes exponentially, year after year.

Diamond Beach is now closed by public consent. If you can't change the action, act to change your conditions. That's a lesson I've taken to heart.

That afternoon, however, I couldn't have guessed what I was in for: the turns in the road were coming too fast. I thought I was wandering down a dusty lane groomed by mild cud-chewing cows. I didn't see the purple clouds gathering low and bleak on the moody horizon. Didn't hear the dogs start to bark when the breeze picked up. Then the storm hit. And I've been buffeted by its winds ever since.

From Celeste: The baby! Underlined. Twice.

It's my shame that makes me hesitate.

But then I hear Madeleine's voice: *Be brave.*

This is what I saw when I walked into the den.

The baby was as lumpy as an abandoned doll limply bent between her brother's legs. I'll never forget Bobby's face at that moment. He was ashen, eyes glazed, and in his hands (even now I can't bear to think of it) he held the baby's brightly marbled intestines as if she'd turned herself inside out, vomited her guts into his lap.

I have no recollection of crossing the room, but there I was at Bobby's side. I sat down gently next to him, tried not to breathe. Bobby was panting, his entire focus on his sister. My children were beyond my reach.

The baby's eyes were wide, her soft wrinkled hands wrapped around her toes. When the cat sniffed her ankle, her foot curled back as the wet nose, then the gentle whiskers, tickled her sensitive skin.

It was the only sign she wasn't a doll as my brave boy started slowly pulling the cotton stuffing from between her lips—a soggy skein of bloated yarn that smelled of rancid yogurt and stale pond water.

But it wasn't her insides. Dear lord. Not her insides.

With enormous care, Bobby tugged and wound the fetid pile of yarn slowly together. Soon, it was a scarlet tuft the size of his fist. Then a waterlogged softball. Still growing. An overripe melon. In no time at all it looked like she'd coughed up a lung, the mass beside him pulsing with mild indifference. When the baby suddenly reached out and slapped it, the bladder shuddered a grotesque reply.

Then Ed walked in like a phantom whose presence makes itself known by the mild creak of a floorboard. My back was turned, but I had no doubt that he'd joined us. All the signs were there. The bark of his scalp. The smelt copper of his authorial armpit. He was standing just outside my peripheral vision, leaning against the molding I'd clutched, white-knuckled, a moment before.

"We need a bucket, Ed. Some rags," I said softly.

My calm was an act. I didn't want to frighten the baby or startle my son's grisly work.

"Hurry." I'm sure I grimaced. "And bring the phone."

He didn't answer. And when Bobby looked at me strangely, I glanced behind me.

There were only three of us in the room.

Then the damn ring of the Royal typewriter sounding off. We all heard it. Ed was upstairs. No doubt about it. Yet I could still smell him. He was right there with us. But nowhere to be seen.

The baby didn't notice my confusion. She didn't struggle as Bobby slowly spooled the yarn from her throat, over her tongue and gums and stubby new teeth. Inch by inch, foot by foot. She didn't gag. Not even once.

How could she not gag?

No doubt because Ed had just written:

She did not gag even once.

Bobby wound the skein around his fist. It was foul and

damp, smelled like spit-up and clotted milk. It was as if the very curd of her was coming undone.

Suddenly there was a small pop, the line came to an end, and, drool running down the back of his wrist, Bobby held up the ulcerated mass in the light. The cat leapt for it. Missed. So the baby yanked her tail. Then belched.

I rocked on my heels. Fell back slowly. Suddenly, the baby and I mirrored each other in limp repose. Her cheeks were fever bright. But mine (I knew without looking) were dusty and drawn. I could taste the sticky weight of my breath. Slowly, I unlocked my jaw, pulled the baby onto my lap.

"Good job, Bobby."

I touched his back, watched his shoulders dip into an angry shrug. With a cough, he climbed back onto the couch.

"Mom?" He was studying me. Without looking, I knew his eyes were full of doubt. Accusation. What could I say to help him understand what had just happened when I had no idea myself?

The baby squirmed contentedly. She was soft. Impossibly warm.

Jittery with life.

CHAPTER SIXTEEN

Threats

Was I crying at Ed's door a few minutes later?

The sounds I made weren't words.

I cursed. I kicked his door. I remember grunting—or was it growling?—as I tried to pry off the knob. Instead, I whispered—my tongue raspy and thick—into the keyhole. My lips were shattered and dry. I tugged off dead skin with my teeth.

"Is this what you want?" I was full of rage. Pure. Simple. I needed to leave my mark on his skin. The way he had left a mark on my life.

My voice wasn't familiar. The tone was shrill. Desperate. It belonged to a wife whom an angry husband had imagined. It didn't belong to me.

"Ed!" He didn't answer. He hadn't answered in days.

"Mom?" Bobby called up from the foot of the stairs. The ball of steamy yarn was sitting now by his foot. The baby rolled it and, from one flight above, I heard it give gently, like a dead fish tested by the bored beak of a gull.

"Everything's all right," I said.

I tried to sound mild, unconcerned, but there was grit in my throat—something hard, unforgiving. They both heard it. A shift in mood, tone, is as palpable as a change of clothes to a child and I watched as the language of their tiny limbs adjusted. Immediately, the baby started to whine. Bobby frowned. The high jinks were over: my boy picked up the ball of wet yarn and, though the baby bleated and moaned, he would not give it to her.

Bobby is his father's son: like Ed, he can hold a grudge.

"Can we go outside?" He sniffed the ball, then looked at me just like he had after his trip to the hospital a month before. The arched brows. The pursed, delicate lips. I was a great source of disappointment to him and, turning up his nose, he let Charlie Parker lick the yarn. It was a feast—both milk and baby—and soon, humpbacked and straining, the cat was begging for more. Bobby at once gave in: pitching the ball out the door, galloping after her as best as he could, his injured leg dragging behind him. In a moment they were gone: the boy clattering into a wall before he lumbered out to the yard; the baby slowly crawling—every inch an uncelebrated victory— behind them.

"Stay on the lawn," I yelled.

It was just a suggestion, and Bobby knew it.

When they were gone, I kicked the door again.

"Ed?" Inside his den, I could hear the remote scratching of pen on paper, the faint creak of his chair as he shifted in place, and I imagined, just for a moment, that he paused and turned, cocked his ear toward the door, listened for my breath on the lock. But it was I who paused, I who listened: I who, bent at the foot of his door, was staring at my bare, stunted toes. Before she died, my mother often said that happy women—by which she meant women who *wished* to be happy (as if dissatisfaction were the predictable result of a woman's misgivings)—cared for their feet, that feet, like the soul, are battered daily and require a tending that is as equally fierce. My mother was engaged seven times, only married once, and I buried her, at her direction, in a new pair of leather pumps she had bought on sale three weeks before her death. "A woman," she wrote to me in her will, "is, like a soldier, prepared for the worst: always own a pair of good shoes."

In my own closet, I knew there was only a tired pair of penny loafers. I'd failed my mother like I'd failed myself. She'd often said as much.

"You," I said to myself, "can be melodramatic," thinking a moment later, that "you" had addressed "I" as though they were quite different people, as though "you" knew "I" better than "I" knew "I," and then it came to me, suddenly—as though "you" had tapped "me" on the shoulder—that perhaps my husband was in fact interfering as I'd begun to suppose. That, inside his office, he'd perhaps written "you can be melo-dramatic" while I stood outside in the hallway: that "I" had not recollected such a thing at all.

In fact, as I very well know—as I've written just a few pages back—my mother is still very much alive. She's been my children's guardian now for three months.

I leave these passages intact as evidence of Ed's continued interference in my life. There's no other reason to keep them.

"Ed!" I pounded on the door, harder this time, but the scratching had stopped. His chair had gone silent. It felt—though I knew better—as if no one, save me, were home.

"Whatever you're doing, you've got to stop, Ed."

What else could I say? I'd try anything.

"Please!"

It doesn't take much to dismantle a door knob. Ed must have heard me working away. He must have known that a screwdriver is both a tool and a weapon.

"Ed?"

He didn't curse as the knob fell to the floor. And when I pushed the door in, he was gone. The window was open: the drapes shimmered in the afternoon breeze. Outside, sitting cross-legged below in the grass, Bobby looked up at me, as the baby beside him kicked her legs in the air. I didn't ask him if he'd seen his father clamber out. I didn't tell him to prevent his sister from eating the freshly bloomed clover. I held my tongue. And Bobby didn't say a word.

It was at that moment I knew I was in real trouble. The kind that can't be cured by packing bags and moving out, hiring a lawyer, or getting divorced.

Since that day, I haven't seen Ed. I haven't smelled him or felt his presence. I haven't even heard his damn typewriter ring.

I was alone. And the only thing I knew for certain was that Ed and I were over.

The message I left for Ed on his desk, scrawled in anger and haste, ended up etched both onto paper as well as the soft wood beneath it. Later, it appeared as Exhibit X in my commitment hearing, a plank of wood cut from his desk, severed from our life—evidence, the Board now says, of "upheaval" in our relationship.

LEAVE MY BABIES ALONE, I'd carved with my ballpoint pen. *TOUCH THEM AGAIN AND I'LL KILL YOU.*

My therapist doesn't give a thing away. Ankles crossed, Madeleine watches me with the same mild detachment with which she no doubt observes her aging golden retriever (framed photo on desk) pass a hard, chalky load in the yard. Aloof, yet mildly jubilant. Ready to don a rubber glove so she can quickly clean up the mess.

It's not that Ed hated babies. Or disliked children in a more general sense. In fact, Bobby's arrival brought about a mild joy, a peace I'd never seen in him before. In the hospital, he held our son lightly—stroked the fragile, sapling shoulders, the bruised, flaring nose—as Bobby gummed in his sleep.

"First generation. Second chance," he said to himself while I dozed in a drug-induced haze. He didn't know I overheard him.

That was long before the memoir began. It took another ten years for him to begin jotting down notes, pinning them to his wall, before starting to write in earnest. This time, as my belly grew in size, he grew more distant: ordering food I could not eat, planning excursions I could not join, even canceling my doctor's appointments. It wasn't that he didn't want the new baby. He just didn't seem to believe a new child was en route: that the shape of our family was about to change.

I thought he'd grow out of it. Adjust.

Eventually, we all adjust.

Not Ed.

CHAPTER SEVENTEEN

The Plot Thickens

In the days after Ed's disappearance, time passed slowly. I found myself anchored in doorways, weighted in chairs. I was sure I had not been abandoned. So I searched for my husband in the backs of closets, in attic cubbies, rapping the walls, looking for hidden seams in the plaster or under floorboards that groaned over hollow spaces below. I fully expected Ed to emerge from a secret room carved from lathe and slat, step from the backbone of our home, where—perhaps—our barley farmer had once hidden a stash of porn, or bar-tab money, from his frugal wife.

Soon, the world inside the farmhouse stopped altogether. Ed was gone. The baby drowsed between naps. Bobby camped out by the stream in our backyard. And though my son came inside for dinner, he resolutely slid his chair from the table as soon as he finished and locked himself up in his room. He answered my questions—*How was school? Do you need help with your homework? How's your leg?* (the same kinds of questions I was leaving for Ed: *How was your day? How is your book going?*

Do you feel OK?)—but Bobby's minimalist parries ("yes," "no," "fine") discouraged elaboration. In no time, talking to my son became no different from not talking to him at all.

It happened so quickly: we no longer spoke *to* each other. We were two people anchored across a divide whose shape we could not name.

We were waiting. Storing our energy.

What for? Celeste wanted an answer I couldn't provide.

Bobby now denies any of this happened. I'm not really surprised.

I now know what we were feeling was dread.

MEMOIR

"What I am writing is something more than mere invention; it is my duty to relate everything about this girl. . . . It is my duty, however unrewarding, to confront her with her own existence."

"I am reminded of certain documents where the true, the secret writing, appears only after chemical treatment, whereby the original, deliberately irrelevant text is revealed to be a pretext."

"I take another note out of the box and try to read the top line, but the handwriting is upside down. I turn it around, but the handwriting is still upside down. Whichever way I turn it, the top line still seems to be upside down."

"She takes my left arm, tells me to make a fist, then open. Make a fist then open again, make the vein appear through the skin blue-green-purple tint to the translucent surface."

"The blood you have lost gathers around you."

"Qui vivra verra, che sera sera, you shall see what you shall see and may the beast man wane."

"I am rising, until my ears explode and begin a long, slow fall at the end of her arm, toward the tile floor."

"A person could be freed by such magic."

One week later, I walked in the door, Bobby hungry and hot on my heels after a long day at school. By the time I set down his backpack and opened the mail, he was already in the refrigerator, his hand on a cold piece of steak.

"Five minutes, Bobby, that's all I need to make dinner."

He shrugged. Now there was a sandwich in one hand, a banana in the other. The window of opportunity was over. Growing boys.

I sighed, tucked the baby into the high chair, gave her a biscuit.

The letter from the IRS was at the bottom of the pile.

COUNTER-MEMOIR

"(So much has been taken from me that loss is a dull if constant, irritation—much like a toothache.)"

"If a physician of high standing, and one's own husband, assures friends and relatives that there is really nothing the matter with one but temporary nervous depression—a slight hysterical tendency—what is one to do?"

"Shall we talk for a moment about the satisfaction of premeditation? The planning, the budgeting, the preparation, the primping! The way girls once, in some other world, must have readied themselves for dates. A slow seduction."

"She goes to a drawer and pulls out the gold scissors."

"When your rage is choking you, it is best to say nothing."

"I may be insane but I protest I'm not feeble-minded."

"Using this knife to cut out the in-between from here to here."

"In other words, only one of us gets out of here alive."

Ed and I were in "error," it claimed. More, it claimed we'd been in error for years: we'd *compounded* the error. The upshot? We owed money: $22,481.62 to be precise.

Would you be surprised to learn that Ed did our taxes? We were in error in so many ways. The taxes didn't begin to cover it.

As I hid the letter so Bobby wouldn't see it, I thought I heard the typewriter ring out upstairs. But when I hurried to Ed's office to look for him, as I'd looked so often before, Ed wasn't there. There was, however, a new stack of pages sitting on his desk.

The manuscript was growing.

CHAPTER EIGHTEEN

The Agreement of Nouns

"Mother," I said on the phone, shortly after my twenty-first birthday. "I think I've found the one."

Ed was in the next room eating a sandwich, a dishtowel tucked into his shirt, a dab of mustard on his nose. At the time, I thought he looked ridiculous and sweet. That was before I had children. Now the sight of bibs, crumbs, and food-streaked faces is a much less endearing sight altogether.

"The one *what*, dear?" She sounded distracted.

Across the room, Ed smiled at me, gesturing, amused, at the mess he'd made.

I'm hopeless, he mouthed.

"I think I'm in love."

There was a pause, a scratch on the line as the phone shifted ears.

"Does he know about Jules?" She tried to sound nonchalant.

It was my turn to pause. "What do you mean?"

She cleared her throat. "Is he interested in you? Or in your brother?"

Was that the moment? my therapist asks.

The moment? I said.

The moment you knew she loved Jules more than you. Madeleine can be frank when she likes.

I choose my words carefully. *She had a lot of things on her mind. She was worried.*

A note in the margins from Celeste: *Be direct. Cast the demons out.*

What an optimist.

"Not everyone is interested in Jules, Mother." Before she could say it, I added: "I am not being naïve."

She cleared her throat. "So you haven't told him."

"He has never asked about Jules," I said.

Her voice was warm in my ear, as though she were standing right beside me.

"Don't you find that odd?"

Did you? Madeleine chimes in.

I didn't talk about Jules, I tell her.

Madeleine's legs bounce a moment. *Jane,* she says, *if you were an amputee and your future mate never talked about your missing leg, how would you feel?*

So you agree with her? I try to sound calm.

(A check mark here from Celeste.)

It's not about "agreement," she says. *We're identifying behaviors.* Madeleine can sit unnervingly still in an uncomfortable plastic chair.

So I had two children with a man who was more interested in my brother than in me. I look up. *Then why didn't Ed leave me when Jules died? Why didn't he leave at the very beginning?*

She nods. *Now,* she says, *we're getting somewhere.*

"Are you there, Jane?" My mother sounded impatient.

"He loves me, Mother."
She clucked her tongue. "Don't tell him anything."
There was a pause.
"Some things are better left unsaid."
Who said that, I now can't recall.
I only remember we didn't say goodbye.
We just quietly hung up our phones.

CHAPTER NINETEEN

The Problem of My Youth

If irony had a flavor, it would taste like steel. Oxidized. Unforgiving. My tongue is rusty from it when I phone my son on Saturday mornings. We get ten minutes. He won't give me five.

"Are you through, Mom?" he says when I tell him I love him.

What can I say? He hangs up. Every week it's the same thing.

When I was a girl, my mother made me feel alone even when we sat at the same kitchen table. Now a locked door separates me from my children. Plexiglass. Fiberoptic cables. A trend can always get worse.

Those you love can always make you feel worse.

From my therapist: *What do you make of that?*

The taste of rust swells, coats my tongue.

I close my eyes so she can't see me rolling them.

I thought I buried "the problem of my youth" (as Celeste likes to call it) in the many yards of the many places I called home since I met Ed. The dorm we filled with books, a futon, a used recliner. Later, a rented house with sloping floors. Then, when Ed joined Hampton, Payne & Lynch LLC, a tony, if compact, apartment seated off an upscale cul de sac not far from the Albright Knox Art Museum. We used to walk its mossy paths while Bobby (a colicky infant then) howled shamelessly from our squeaky stroller, much to the art lovers' dismay.

They glared. Ed laughed. His audacity once amused me.

Our last home was the farmhouse. Most finally, the farmhouse.

We will never move into the home I imagined now. The home Ed promised. The one thing I've always wanted. The one thing, it seems, I can never have.

The past is the lens through which you observe the present. The one lesson I've learned—perhaps the only lesson I've ever learned—is that your perspective rarely changes unless you first want it to change. Then take direct action for change. But only eyesight changes easily. Which is to say: over time, it gets worse.

My therapist rustles her chair. I sense her mind shifting. The movement is as perceptible as her hand reaching up to push a strand of hair behind her ear.

"Let's discuss your brother today." It's not a suggestion.

Should have seen it coming.

"You mean 'the problem of my youth'?"

She cocks her head and, for a moment, resembles the photograph of the golden retriever sitting on her desk.

I clarify. "That's what my lawyer calls it."

"And you?"

I shrug. "The problem wasn't mine. The problem was given to me. You might say: the problem became mine."

"Tell me." The naugahyde chair slides against her linen pants.

"There are newspaper articles about him you can read," I suggest. "Op-eds. Three dissertations at last count." I study her. "You don't need me."

"Remember," she says, "I want to hear *your* story." She pauses. "Not his. Not hers."

Her voice is as soft as velvet on an infant's cheek.

"Tell me," she says again.

So I do.

CHAPTER TWENTY

An Articulation of Flesh

"Dad was looking for you today."

The baby had been home from the hospital for just a few weeks, and Bobby said it without inflection, as though I was the one who had disappeared. Not his father.

It can't be hard to imagine my surprise.

I tried to mimic his deadpan expression. Seem nonchalant. I let my knees slacken, slouch. Bad idea: I suddenly looked herniated, desolate, like a marionette abandoned by a puppeteer on a coffee break.

Bobby wasn't impressed.

"I was here all day with your sister," I said as casually as I could, my forearm swinging loose from my elbow. "I wonder how your dad missed me." I pretended to smile.

Bobby nodded. Then looked at me thoughtfully. "He seems distracted lately. Just like you." Already, he was pouring himself a glass of juice, chattering on as though he'd been thinking about his parents on the walk home and had come to an important conclusion. "I think it's his book. It's tiring, he said, to write it. Though he thinks he's almost done."

The baby stirred and I rubbed her belly in her bassinet. "He did, did he?" I tried not to sound miffed. "How much more time does he need?"

Bobby mashed his lips around a cookie, and when he spoke, a batter of dough and saliva foamed on his lips, but I didn't bother to hand him a napkin.

"Something about two more weeks. Dad said to be patient, that everything would be better after that."

It was too much that Ed would use our son as a messenger. Too much that he hadn't told me about his book himself.

It was all just too much.

Humiliation was thick in my throat but I broke down, posed the question Ed surely wanted me to ask.

"Did you believe him?" There was a crystal edge in my voice.

Bobby looked startled. The baby mewled. I forget sometimes that, while Bobby has secrets, he's still young enough to believe that his parents do not.

"Never mind," I said quickly, course-correcting before he could answer. I had a sudden inspiration. "Maybe we'll name your sister when he's done, too."

Bobby set his glass down on the counter. He wouldn't meet my gaze.

"Dad says he settled on Sophie, after grandmamma. The one I never met."

He studied at me carefully, much more carefully than a boy ought.

"Dad said you agreed with him. I've been calling her Sophie for days now. That's what my friends call her now too."

My face stretched. I made a convincing smile for him. An act no child can appreciate.

After a moment, Bobby raced out the back door to go stomp in the brook, and I was left with "Sophie" alone, as I often was, curdling her milk on my blouse.

CHAPTER TWENTY-ONE

Ever-Deepening Shade

After the butter knife incident, I'd quiz Bobby about his day as soon as he returned from school: how his leg felt, what his friends said, if he had homework. He'd answer briefly, then go to his room, shut the door. He didn't notice how much I wanted to talk, or how I was changing. In the bathroom mirror, my eyes looked hollow. My skin was blue, hypoxiated. But it was hard to get my son to sit still. To get him to elaborate the current frame of his life.

One day I tried a different tactic.

"Have you seen your father recently?" I asked as he walked through the door and set down his bag. There was a plate of cookies on the table and, as I'd planned, he went straight for them. Wolfed one down, reached for another. I didn't stop him. They would keep him near me in the kitchen without having to ask him to stay.

Bobby chewed. Gave me a quizzical look. Was he judging me, I wondered? How long had he been able to see through my ruses?

"Of course," he said. "We see him every day." He leaned over and blew on "Sophie's" hair softly. "You know that."

I did?

Did you? the Board asks.

Of course not, I tell them. But that wasn't the dilemma I faced at that moment. What I suddenly realized was that Ed's efforts had already expanded imperceptibly outward. His work had not only reshaped our spousal relationship—one now based on absence, on negation—but it had also begun to alter my rapport with Bobby. At that moment, it manifested itself in my inability to ask a simple question: to divulge to my child what I did not know.

In the face of my child's complicity, I was powerless.

Where did you see your father? I wanted to ask him. *In what room? How did he look? What did he do?* Which is to say, I wanted to ask: *Do you know what your father wants?*

Instead, I held my tongue. Tamped its tip between my teeth until it bled. An articulation of flesh, not sound.

Bobby smiled and left the room with the entire plate of cookies.

I didn't say a word.

CHAPTER TWENTY-TWO

That Old Line

I

"Hello, Mother," I said when she answered her phone. I was determined to stay calm.

"Jane?" She sounded surprised to hear my voice.

"It's been a long time." My most agreeable tone.

I could easily picture her as she leaned into the iPhone, her hard jaw and prominent forehead jutting out as squarely as a birdhouse over the slender post of her neck.

Nothing for a moment, then:

"Is something wrong with Ed, dear?"

How did she know?

I kept my voice steady.

"He's disappeared, Mother."

A long pause. Then:

"What did you do?"

"Excuse me?" My tone was sharp. I couldn't help it.

She thought I didn't hear her clearly.

"What did you do *to make him leave?*" It sounded like she was hissing in my ear.

I snapped.

"What did *you* do to make my father leave?"

I heard a cat yowl in the background as she stepped on its tail. Then a definitive click.

A few weeks later, my house was on fire. And I was standing at the curb, my son beside me, my daughter cupped in my arms, watching my memories smolder.

II

"Hello, Mother," I said when she answered the phone, a few days before the police knocked on my door. For a moment, she didn't respond.

"Is it you?" she said.

"Ed," I explained, "has gone missing. Just like Dad."

I heard her adjust the phone, pull it tight to her ear. Perhaps she was losing her hearing.

"Say again?" she said.

"I haven't seen Ed in six weeks."

"The part about your father," she said.

"Ed has disappeared," I repeated. "Just like Dad disappeared when we were kids."

She coughed. "Your father didn't disappear, dear."

I chose my words more carefully.

"He left us."

There was long pause. I could hear her sucking softly on her gums over the phone line.

"Sweetheart," she began again, "your father died in a car accident on the way home from work. You were at the funeral."

"For God's sake, Mother," I said. "Not that old lie."

She didn't miss a beat:

"You've always believed what you wished to believe."

Before I could stop myself, I threw my phone across the room. The screen shattered. The line went dead. Once again, I was alone.

Part I. SPOONS

—as in "Born with a silver spoon in his mouth"

The Romans designed two types of spoon. The oval-shaped *ligula* was used for soft foods like soup. The rounder *cochleare*—derived from the word for "spiral-shaped snail shell"—was used for eating shellfish and eggs. All subsequent English spoons are based on this early Roman design. The past reveals itself in our most common domestic objects. We are who we have always been.

Part II. FORKS

—as in "Stick a fork in it"

The word *fork* derives from *furca*, the Latin word for "pitchfork." By the seventh century A.D., the fork had become common in royal households in the Middle East. Three centuries later, the fork arrived in wealthy Byzantium homes. Yet when Maria Argyropoulina, Greek niece of Byzantine Emperor Basil II, tried to introduce Venice to the fork in 1004—having brought a case of golden forks for her wedding to the doge's son—she was at once condemned for heresy. "God, in his wisdom, has provided man with natural forks, his fingers," one clergyman wrote. Maria Argyropoulina's death not long after from plague was widely viewed at the time as divine intervention.

It took three more centuries to popularize the fork in Europe. It didn't arrive in England until 1611. The man who introduced it—Thomas Coryat of Odcombe—was known afterwards by the nickname "Furcifer," which technically means "fork-bearer," but was also a pun.

At the time, a *furcifer* was a man doomed to hang.

Part III. KNIVES

—as in "X-Acto"

The earliest knives (3000 B.C.E.) were shaped from obsidian or flint through a process called "knapping"—the flaking and chipping away at a rock until a blade is formed. Knife artifacts have been found in the ruins of every culture.

You might say, where humans are, knives have always been too.

Knives are complicated status symbols. Both kings and criminals, for instance, once presented their knives as a sign of bravery. Yet students of modern etiquette know that knives should not be given to newly wedded couples. It suggests the marriage will be unhappy or come to a violent end.

In 2005, a group of physicians in England proposed a prohibition against long (but not short) kitchen knives in order to reduce violent crime. Long knives, they wrote, "have little practical value in the kitchen."

Lesson 1
Do not eat—with spoons, forks, or knives—when tired.
Do not eat—with spoons, forks, or knives—in bed.

Lesson 2
At any time, a utensil may become a weapon.

CHAPTER TWENTY-THREE

Eat This, Not That

When my neighbor Joy Westin showed up on my doorstep I barely registered that her overplucked eyebrows were stitched into a knot, a thread I wished I could pull to watch her entire face unravel.

In her hand, she held a limp plastic bag out and away from her body. There was something small and dead inside. A rodent.

What I noticed? That Joy's shorts were not just pressed. They'd been starched too. Good grief. Who starches clothes anymore?

The potted ferns I'd sold her were fine, she said, without saying hello. "Your cat's continued fondness for them, however, has become a nuisance." That's exactly how she put it. Evidently, Bobby's cat, Charlie Parker, was delivering to Joy's porch the tiny lifeless gifts she had once brought to ours.

"Perhaps," I said, "the scent on the ferns is throwing her off?"

Joy bared her teeth. "Best do something," she said, shaking the baggie, "or . . ." She shrugged, and the twinge of her padded shoulders insinuated a whole host of barbarities.

She tossed the baggie at my feet. Inside, the dead mouse's mouth was open. Its tiny pink nose looked sweet and unobjectionable over the gash in its neck where feline teeth had nipped and tucked with ferocious artistry.

"Let's be reasonable," I began, but she cut me off.

"If you'll do nothing," she said, her voice rising, "I'll speak to your husband."

Joy was the kind of woman who presented her chin the way a bull displays its horns.

She stood very still, her knees bent. Panting.

Normally I would have tried to appease her.

Normally.

Upstairs, the typewriter rang out. She didn't move. Clearly, she hadn't heard it.

"You do that," I said, picking the bag off my doorstep. "Talk to Ed. Tell him all about it." I paused, smiled. "Every detail. The next time you see him."

She looked mildly surprised. Satisfied even.

I smiled. But for a much different reason.

After I shut the door, I took a bath.

It was the first time I'd felt good in weeks.

CHAPTER TWENTY-FOUR

Yes

When I was a girl, I loved as a girl. The world spun on its expected axis: gravity, magnetism pulsing the planet through each inevitable rotation. On the ground, I was driven by less predictable forces. Hormones. Pheromones. Not to mention sugar, alcohol. Caffeine too. I was a tiny thing then, bone-thin, and always cold. While Ed was hardy, a survivor, a young man in his prime, and when he held me—his body wrapped around me as if he were a blanket—I heated up, my whole world went right. I became moist, happy, as he pulled off my clothes, laid into me, a silent vigil. There was no need for declarations.

Back then, I took his silence for sincerity. We were beyond words.

Ed was my center. The n in my algebraic equation. He made my world make sense.

It occurs to me years later that had I been more weighty—in pounds, I mean—Ed might not have impressed me so much.

If I'd carried my own weight, I wouldn't have needed his warmth as much as I did. My life would have been different. His too. Maybe he wouldn't have needed to write that book. So I wouldn't have needed to write mine either.

The last time I saw Ed—which is to say, the Ed I knew—I was six months pregnant and already unsteady on my hot, swollen feet. It was a quiet afternoon, the house was a disaster, and I was rummaging in the cabinets trying to sort them out before Bobby returned from school. There was a platter on a top shelf I could not reach. Maybe a jar wouldn't open. Perhaps a pilot light went out. The predictable perils of a domestic landscape.

What specific event prefaced my shout to him is less important than the way he answered.

I called for him. I was tired, and it was too damn hard to climb the stairs. The second time I called, he came out of his den. He was wearing gym shorts, his t-shirt tucked into their elastic waist. From below, I could tell his clothes were dirty, covered in ink stains. Or toner. Maybe coffee or jam. His hair was standing on end and his skin looked waxy, as if at any moment it might peel off and drip down onto me at the foot of the stairs. I couldn't help it, I took a step back.

Ed looked like he was dissolving. Vaporizing slowly into a new plasmic state.

He didn't seem to notice.

"I need you, Ed." I'm sure I sounded urgent. But he just stood there, looking at me. He scratched his head, then his belly gently. Absentmindedly. He tried to meet my gaze. Took a breath.

Then exhaled it.

What he intended to say, I'll never know. But it was there between us—his breath like his meaning—suspended somewhere between the first and second floors of the farmhouse, an invisible cloud hanging there in the stairwell.

There are many different kinds of weather inside and outside a home.

"Yes," he said with something like pity in his voice. "Yes." Now sounding farther away. "Yes, yes, yes." He wasn't angry but, like a child testing out a word for its meaning, he seemed to be questioning what the word "yes" meant. If "yes" were an acknowledgment or an obligation. And if "yes" always meant "yes" or carried a history with it: a "yes" that arose from a previous "maybe" or perhaps from a "no," perhaps a "no" that had been changed to a "yes," which is to say, a "no" misunderstood as a "yes," or a "yes" that didn't mean "yes" any longer because it carried all the "no's" before it that had been turned inside out, their meaning repealed, because of the prior weight they carried.

"Yes."

The last time, he said it firmly, the pale flesh of his mouth firming up like an egg white against the heat of a pan.

That's when I knew Ed really meant "no." That's when he turned, went back to his den, and began to type on the machine he'd found in our attic.

I never saw my Ed again.

Before the Board inquires further—*When you say "never," Jane, what do you precisely mean?*—let me qualify my words. Disappearances aren't as black and white as the word suggests. They're as much about the devastating presence of absence as the interminable absence of presence—qualities that are not opposed, though their interrelation is often ignored. How often have you apologized—for instance, during an important meeting or conversation—for being "somewhere else," even though you were standing right there, ears attuned, gaze locked on the speaker before you?

Ed's "disappearance" occurred in phases, the last stage being the most definitive. I haven't seen him now in a year.

Yet I'm reminded of his absence every day: Ed's absence is appallingly present.

For six more months, I did in fact occasionally "see" Ed—which is to say, a man who looked like Ed and acted like Ed, a man who even demonstrated many of the qualities that had made Ed "Ed" for me historically: his easy smile, the (now) almost imperceptible hitch in his stride, the way he wrung his hands like an old woman when he was otherwise still. But something was off, remained a half step out of phase. Sure, he wandered into the kitchen to make himself coffee (milk and three sugars). He even wandered out again as he was accustomed to doing, his mug dripping a path on the carpet from the kitchen up to his den. He still mussed Bobby's hair, piled plates in the sink, and fed Charlie Parker when we forgot. He even opened the mail and sorted it for us: junk mail on the bottom, bills on the top, personal correspondence in a stack of its own.

For all intents and purposes, the man with whom I lived should have been Ed. So I failed to notice the new man growing beneath Ed's skin like a bush sprouting new branches after it's been pruned. He was the old Ed. But he'd begun to take on a much different shape.

Which is to say, Ed was going for a long time before he was gone. And he was gone for a while before he disappeared fully. It's not just a question of tense: it's a question of tension. I felt the latter. But the former—that my husband could exist in a past tense while present in our marriage—didn't occur to me until too late. Until I couldn't find my husband any longer. And he disappeared for good.

And when was that, please? The Board is very polite. But they don't hear a single word.

"Not long after we moved into the new old house." The house that was rebuilt after the fire at our home insurer's direction. Part farmhouse, part new addition. A cobbled-together, mixed-up home that barely looked like its former self. Much like me.

One day Ed was there.
The next day he was gone.

Lately, Celeste has begun to complain that while my book has achieved its initial objective, it no longer offers anything useful to my case. *There is an absence of landscape,* she says. *Real time. Daily life. Show us how you lived with Ed, your children. Show us what you've lost.*

I want to please her. I want to do as she says.

Yes, I say, taking a lesson from Ed.

Something shifts in her face, a tiny crack inside a block of ice. I know that look. I've felt it on my own face before.

Celeste understands I really mean "no."

A list of loss for Madeleine and Celeste:

The baby's damp palms. Her oatmeal-caked chin. The paste of milk behind her ears. The fine hair, now thick. Her hiccupped laugh. The open mouth, wide, demanding. Later, sweetly gumming my cheek. The heat of her thighs. Sharp nails on my chest. The tiny hands clasping my ankles, knees, breasts, hair. Pulling. Her head on my arm. The pulse of her breath. Small, unscuffed shoes. The dimpled arms. Her "no." Her sigh. Her first word. *Ball.* The words before the first words. The simple sounds whose meaning only I knew.

Bobby's long legs, the smooth plain of his belly, his scrub of hair, never combed. His needs. His howls. The perpetual frown. Dead worms. Dirt. Toilet paper. Blocks. Joy that is anger. Anger, joy.

I am the last leaf on a deciduous tree. Hanging on. Already dead. In time, swept away by the wind.

I can no longer feel myself breathe, though I hear myself breathing.

A list is always incomplete.

Strangler Figs

In botanical study, *strangler figs*—the common name for a variety of tropical plants and vines—share a common growth pattern adapted to the darkest forests where light is scarce. Seedlings begin their lives as *epiphytes*—plants that develop on other plants—then strategically grow in two directions: downward, the vines coiling ever more tightly around the host tree, and upward, reaching toward the sunlight. In effect, as the plant grows, it chokes or "strangles" the tree which supports it, and gives it shape.

Eventually, a mature strangler fig will fully envelope the original host tree. In time, the host tree then dies and the strangler fig becomes a column-shaped tree with a completely hollow center.

Male genitalia have been, at one time or another, referred to as figs. Generally, figs refer to the testicles.

Not surprisingly, "strangling fig" behavior can be identified among "fauna" as well.

It is particularly visible in long-term human relationships.

Strangler Fig Species

Ficus aurea, also known as the Florida Strangler Fig.

Ficus barbata, also known as the Bearded Fig.

Ficus gibbosa, also known as Humped Fig.

Ficus tamlinsa, also known as the Husband Fig

Ficus virens, also known as the White Fig.

Ficus watkinsiana, also known as the Nipple Fig.

CHAPTER TWENTY-FIVE

Confession

Did I kill Ed?

Of course I killed him. He said so himself.

You're killing me.

He liked to say that a lot.

You're just killing me, Jane.

He'd say it with a straight face, shake his head, then slowly walk off to the den. If you go by his count, I killed him so many times it's impossible to keep up.

Choke on it, I'd sometimes say. *Go choke.*

But I did not take out his eyes with an oyster fork.

Or drop a laptop in the bath during a long soak after work.

I did not make him an antifreeze cocktail to ward off the Buffalo winter.

Or garrote him with shoelaces as he dozed at his desk.

I did not push him over the loose railing he'd always promised to fix.

Or cut the brake line on the Volvo. (I don't know a thing about cars.)

I did not crack his head with a hammer. A crowbar. Not even a wrench.

The nail gun is—right there—by the tool box. The pickaxe still sits rusting in the garage.

The ropes? They're still piled together, a mess of moldering knots.

And the kitchen knives—all of them—line up side by side in their cracked wooden block.

Of course I killed Ed.

But he disposed of the body.

When you find him, you'll see.

CHAPTER TWENTY-SIX

Trust Your Senses

When the end came—as the end always must—it arrived simply. There were no outbursts, no car chases. No quick dashes for the exit.

There was a sigh. But no real surprise.

I woke up from an afternoon nap one Wednesday afternoon not long after the school year had begun. I'd slept upright with the baby and she was plastered against my shoulder. Down the hall, I could hear Ed's typewriter clacking away in his office while the birds chattered outside. A fan whirred. Some chimes on the porch tinkled when the occasional late summer breeze puffed against them. Everything was as it should be.

Right?

But then, as the baby stirred and the typewriter rang out, it was as if my hearing suddenly improved—as if, unexpectedly, I could perceive subtle intonations in the sounds outside: the fear in a robin's carefree song, the blood in a terrier's yap, the lust in the creak of a gate. The baby woke, and I put these subtleties from my mind. But they did not fade, and I began to listen more closely to what was said around me. To every word spoken. A heartbeat of syllables. The sonic frequency of our home.

From that moment on, I could hear the chemical hum of our thoughts. Hear Ed already leaving me. Before he'd even risen from his desk.

The police didn't come when I hoped they would come, when I needed them to pound on my door, take a look in Ed's office to assure me that everything would be just fine. No one came when Bobby was hurt. Or the baby. No one asked after Bobby when he started to sleepwalk at night, wandering down the hall, then the stairs to the kitchen, where he'd sit at the table, in the same chair where he'd been hurt months before. *It's OK*, I'd say, chafing his hands, leading him back to his room. *We're all right.* You're *all right.*

Bobby never answered, just rubbed his eyes, pushed me off roughly, then trudged back up the stairs. When he woke up in the morning, he'd complain that his slippers weren't where he'd left them.

What did you do? he'd say before he brushed his teeth, shaking himself from a fug of sleep. I'd explain what happened. But he always complained I'd made the whole thing up.

In hindsight, I now realize he thought that about a lot of things.

There is nothing more dreadful than a child's doubt.

Are we lost, Mom? he often asked as we drove through town, even if we'd taken a familiar road—to school, to the market, to the doctor's office. He meant something else, that's evident now. But as we sped along the freshly paved boulevards, I'd reassure him that we were on track, that everything was as it was supposed to be. That we had each other.

He'd nod at that. What he imagined was happening to him, to me—to his father—I'll never know. I've come to accept that now.

When the police finally came, it was Regina who brought them to my door.

As I opened it, I studied their odd triangulation on my front step.

"Regina, you've brought friends."

Of course they weren't my friends. Regina wasn't my friend. But they allowed her to take the children over to her house for dinner while they questioned me.

"Someone has to look for Ed," she said that day. "You should have called the police days ago." She looked around, took in the curtains drawn over the windows. Then she was gone. And I was left with two officers in their sturdy square shoes weighing down my farmhouse floor.

She's fucking my husband, I said, when they noted that Ed hadn't been heard from for days. Maybe weeks.

Maybe longer.

Why didn't I call my lawyer at once? The only lawyers I knew were from Ed's practice. How could I call them? Whose side would they be on?

So I foolishly offered the truth.

"He's disappeared," I said. "One day Ed was here, the next day he wasn't. Bobby says he's seen him. Me?" My neck broke against the heat of the moment. "I've looked for him . . . No luck."

No one can accuse me of changing my story. On the particulars, I've always been firm.

The officers asked other questions. Bobby's injury came up. I did my best to explain how the knife had slipped—yet again. They nodded, took notes, then politely asked to look in

Ed's office. Why would I deny them? Maybe they'd find a clue where I had not.

The light, shining in the east window, was hitting the desk just right as we walked into the office. In the glare, beside Ed's idle typewriter, my threat—the words I'd unintentionally etched into the wood weeks before—were set off in bold relief. My accusations. My anger. My hurt.

The officers stared at the desk, taking it all in, before turning back to me where I hovered in the doorway. My jaw was strung together with feather and string. I could not keep it shut.

That's when their collective uniformed gaze drifted from me to the door itself, to the busted scratched doorknob. Clearly, someone had removed the knob, then reattached it.

Someone had broken in from the hall.

A light flared up in their eyes. They sized me up. What would I look like in the middle of the night, a hefty screwdriver in my hand? Maybe a knife? Perhaps just an oversized serving fork?

They didn't handcuff me when they brought me in for questioning. But they did tuck me into the back seat of the patrol car behind a cage. An air freshener on the dashboard gave off the gritty scent of cinnamon. But it couldn't dispel the stale smell of old shoes and despair. It was awfully hard to breathe.

On their porches, my neighbors watched. Regina stood in the middle of the street, her hand on her hips. Bernard's Lexus steered clear of her as he drove out of the neighborhood. Celeste tells me he hasn't been back. Not since he found out she was sleeping with Ed.

The farmhouse is shuttered now. But it will soon be razed. After the fire, and the subsequent rebuild, the Clarence Center Historical Society deemed its value too uneven to justify the continued legal costs. After salvaging some wood, tools from the basement, a cedar room where the farmers had once cured ham, they dropped the case to preserve my last home. I've been told they made an exhibit from what they've called the "reclaimed residuals" of the farmhouse. My neighbors eventually got their way.

As the patrol car drove me off, martini glasses clinked on my neighbors' porches. I didn't need to see them to know they were there.

Trusting our eyes, after all, is the most significant mistake the human species makes.

For instance, Ed is still here.

Can't you tell?

A Marcescent Limb

In this place, I have no dreams. I thank the Board for that. Sometimes Madeleine. But mostly my friends Lithium, Lunesta, and Seroquel. After supper, I dress for bed, accept my Dixie cup dosage when the nurse stops in for Bed Check #1. I have one hour before she returns, one hour to write down my thoughts as I hide under the sheets before the meds kick in. Right on schedule, she returns for Bed Check #2 and dims the lights. By then, I've hidden my pencil, my paper. I'm beginning to drift into the shadows, my mind closing down like a city shop door at dusk, eyelids growling for the floorboards. After that, there's no going back. Eight hours later, the lights creep back up, and so do I. There's no night anymore. The stars fail to align. I can't remember Bed Checks #3, #4, or #5. The nurses creeping in with their stale breath and rubber-soled shoes.

There are signs. My bathrobe has shifted on its chair. A small plant on the sill has been turned toward the light. The vent cover is awry on its half-stripped screws. I am not the first to hide keepsakes behind it: a ChapStick, a wad of soft tissues, a small red leaf tracked in on a doctor's shoe.

I know I won't be the last.

The nurses let me keep these small objects. Madeleine has told them (Celeste has revealed) that "an element of privacy, of secrecy, is healthy for the healing mind." And as my keepsakes pose no danger, the nurses just monitor the growing collection. What it tells them—how Madeleine interprets the mild, seemingly indiscriminate stash—I have no idea. After all, I'm not supposed to know that they know it's there. So the secret hangs between us like an unspoken thought. That's nothing new for me.

What Madeleine really wants is a look at my book. But the nurses don't know about the loose molding where I've hidden it, the pages rolled up and secreted behind the toe-beaten fascia, concealed within an unseen architecture of wood stud and drywall. The farmhouse taught me simple things about lathe and molding. Above all, how to conceal what our home inspector once called "problem areas" with a bit of spit, damp tissue, and ChapStick. Wouldn't the nurses be surprised?

As I adjust the vent, I tap the molding gently with my toe. No need to look down.

Solid.

Only Celeste knows where I've hidden this book. Only she knows what it says. She is the only person I trust.

Stretching my pasty unshaven legs—no razors allowed even in the low-risk ward—I shuffle back into the loose clothes that serve as daywear at the Institute. Like the sleep meds and the anti-anxiety pills, my routine, I've learned, is another kind of prescription. The nurses get you hooked on the pattern until your body betrays you, wakes you up for a fix at 6 a.m., when all I used to crave at that time of day was more sleep or a hot cup of coffee.

I've changed—wrong tense—*been* changed in so many ways. If you can't change the action, act to change your conditions. Didn't I say I took that lesson to heart? I can adapt to life at BPI. To the loss of my husband. Even to the loss of my case. Celeste has assured me: *There will be a time for review.* Her statement is open-ended. Perhaps I can even adjust to the future tense.

What I can't do? Adjust to the loss of my children.

So I will adjust my life.

Since I can't dream at night, I'll dream during the day. A dream that is common, simple, even true. A dream of everyday life. A dream at a window over a cracked concrete lot. Below, the staff's collection of rusty, dinged cars. Beyond, a scruff of young trees.

A dream of the days before the Board.

Before Madeleine and Celeste.

A dream of supermarkets and shoe stores. Overrun closets and crabgrass plots. Of post office clerks. Dental hygienists. Blinking yellow lights. Cavernous slush-filled potholes cratering strip-mall parking lots. The places I once spent my time trafficking clamshelled toys and canisters of apple juice. With my children. Their noses in an unruly state of secretion. Demanding this toy. This treat. This ride.

This. Now. Please.

Where was Ed? Nowhere to be seen. My dream accounts for this too.

The treeless plateau outside a big-box store was heaven then. The smell of tar rising from the pavement in summer. Hot gum on the soles of my sneakers. A squeaky, broken-wheeled cart. Bobby used to ride on the back, hanging on by one finger. Hair in his eyes—a shoelaced peril—while the baby hiccupped and squirmed in her car seat as I pushed. The baby's eyes on me. Always on me. Making sure I was there.

Back at the car, I strap them in. Check all the latches and belts.

"Here," I tell Bobby. "This is for you. Because you are my first, my good boy. Because you are fierce, and my joy."

He rolls his eyes. Then takes the package from my hands.

In a moment, the plastic is in his teeth. He rips and tugs—his canines have evolved for this—and he eventually peels from the transparent shell a remote-controlled plane. A car that talks. A BB gun. A bow and arrow. A puppy. A personal robot. A bounce house. A battery-powered car. A rocket booster. A ray gun. My bright shining love.

"Wow," he says flatly. But I know he's impressed.

The baby, meanwhile, chews on the ear of her winsome new bunny.

Behind us, all the cars are gone. And so are the people. It's just the kids and me and a shopping cart with four new oiled wheels on the perfectly repaved parking lot.

"Bobby," I say, looking at the cart, unbuckling him as though we'd just arrived.

I don't need to say more. He's already by me, already sailing. Pumping his lean, strong legs, running and screeching and hopping on the front of the cart as it sails, his t-shirt aloft.

The strip mall, our island, in the vast dark sea around us.

I want nothing more.

Outside my window, a sudden shift in the weather.

Beyond the door, a small sound in the night.

A draft is always incomplete

Afterword

An Open Case

At the time of *Choke Box*'s publication, Jane Boward Tamlin continues to be listed as "missing, presumed dead." Lieutenant Earl Jaffe of the CBPD—who now works her cold-case file—believes she likely met her end at the hands of her lawyer Celeste Price or her therapist Madeleine Hogue while at the Buffalo Psychiatric Institute. Jaffe fully rejects (1) the "release order" in Boward's BPI file as a patent forgery, and also (2) remains "intrigued," he says, by the possibility of either (husband) Edward Tamlin's or (mother) Helena Boward's involvement in Jane's disappearance. It is now known that Price and Hogue cultivated, and tried to profit from, Jane's unfinished manuscript. Hard evidence of further criminal involvement, however, has never come to light. Jaffe has speculated that the manuscript sale may have merely been a crime of opportunity that clouds the facts of the case.

What is known? Jane Boward Tamlin was last seen sitting in her bed at BPI during the evening medication check. On her chart, her mood was described as "normal" (i.e., "dour") by BPI Nurse Rollins. In the morning, Jane was gone. A vent cover had been knocked askew on its screws. Jane's bathrobe—discovered tossed on the floor—led investigators to initially believe it was hastily, or violently, removed. But there was no blood or other significant DNA found at the scene.

Jane had simply disappeared.

Time Line

Choke Box was originally submitted to CounterSeed Press (publisher of all of Jules Boward's books) with a cover letter "signed" by Jane Boward Tamlin: she was writing, she claimed, "from an undisclosed location while on the lam." Several email exchanges followed. "Time was of the essence," the author insisted. One week later, CounterSeed Press issued a six-figure check to a post-office box in northeastern Ohio. Three weeks later, as accelerated meetings about marketing and production began, a leak about the forthcoming book was posted to a Jules Boward's fan forum, "JBlog." The new book, fans speculated, might shed light on his peculiar death. Interest was intense.

Twelve weeks after that, Celeste Price and Madeleine Hogue were arrested for fraud. Grainy video shows a mildly irritated Celeste Price eyeing an officer who is holding her by the elbow. Photos of Madeleine Hogue are grimmer. There is blood spatter on her shirt. As one caption explains, "Sigmund"—Madeleine's golden retriever—had lunged at two plainclothes officers at the dog park. One moment, Sig was humping a poodle half his size behind a darkhearted nettle bush. The next, his brains were being flushed down a storm drain while the other pups—tails tucked and howling—were escorted by their owners quickly home. It has been proposed that the still missing Edward Tamlin may have orchestrated his wife's disappearance. Given what Jane implied (revealed?) about Jules Boward and his books, an alternate theory—that Helena Boward ended her own daughter's life—remains of significant popular, if currently unfounded, interest. In fact, Helena Boward's eventual agreement with CounterSeed Press not to contest this manuscript's publication (after a year of legal wrangling) has been described as a "generous settlement" by her estate, under the circumstances. Insider analysts are more circumspect: to them, Helena Boward's decision was a typically sound, even savvy, business decision. As one review noted, the controversy over Jane's self-styled *counter-memoir* has "refreshed all Jules Boward book sales with a new audience of surly adolescents and their overanxious parents."

Helena Boward's most recent act was less auspicious: less than a year after Jane's disappearance, she petitioned the Erie County's Eighth Judicial District Court to declare her daughter dead in absentia.

The petition was tabled due to insufficient documentation. The case is still listed as "open."

Boward Herstory

Jane Marie Boward Tamlin was born in Cherry Hill, New Jersey, on July 15, 1982, to James Boward (copy editor) and Helena Marchant (sales clerk). Three years later, on August 22, 1985, the family welcomed a son, Jules, to their small garden apartment on Grove Boulevard, not far from the creamy sumac fields that choke Playwicki State Park. In the early years (1982–1987), the Boward family was wholly unremarkable—healthy, suburban, middle class. Records indicate that James Boward worked across the Schuylkill River at the now defunct *Philadelphia Daily News*, while Helena Boward took occasional retail work at midscale women's clothing stores. There is little to suggest, in short, that from this hub of extraordinary unexceptionalism two writers of note would mark literary scholarship: the young phenom often known as "J.B." to his international readership, and his sister Jane who, a decade after her brother's death, has now claimed his books as her own.

The Boward family saga began in 1989 with the disappearance[1] of Jane's and Jules's father. At the time, the siblings were seven and four respectively. As fourteen-year-old J.B. wrote at length in his first memoir, *Living with Mother*, the household became increasingly volatile after their father's desertion. Dominated by a mother who, clinicians now speculate, required intervention for an undiagnosed psychiatric condition, the children were regularly, if unpredictably, uprooted—moving to new apartments and school districts on average every four months. Family life was rocky. Friends were scarce. It's not too much to say that the Boward family was in trouble.

As J.B. reflects in *Living with Mother:* "Math is shit. My mom + 2 kids = 0 family at all."

Published when J.B. was just fourteen years old, *Living with Mother* was embraced initially as a "postmodern bildungsroman" by editor Howard M. Davies, who described it as a "coming of age story in which the protagonist never grows up." The book offered what he went on to call "a real-time view of insipid adolescence" neglected by classical

---

1. Official documents are incomplete. Researchers have discovered a New Jersey marriage license in the names of Helena Marie Marchant and James Edward Boward dated August 15, 1979. However, the birth date listed on the marriage license for James Boward does not match the birth certificates for any U.S.-born James Edward Boward on file.

treatments of the genre. Documenting J.B.'s family troubles with his premature (arguably preternatural) cultural observations in a voice marked by minimalist flair and a precociously limited adolescent vocabulary, Jules was quickly declared by *BAM! Magazine*'s Warton Coe: the "first reality TV star of the printed word." In no time at all, Jules was something of a celebrity.

Davies's marketing team at first positioned the memoir for a young adult audience. But Gen X parents struggling with the Y2K event horizon quickly turned to J.B.'s work as a resource for understanding wayward teens. Today, *Living with Mother* continues to be shelved in both the young adult and parenting sections at local big-box book retailers.

It has never gone out of print.

Janey

Throughout J.B.'s all too brief career, his older sister "Janey" avoided the limelight. In her brother's memoirs, she is presented as aloof and unavailable, physically away at school, and emotionally distant from the domestic entanglements of J.B.'s daily life. She appears most regularly in depictions of his early childhood as the jealous and moody alternative to his charmingly boyish antics. In *Living with Mother,* for instance, her appearances are regularly accompanied by the leitmotif of a slammed door, followed by the syncopated cluck and chip of the once revolutionary video game Pong: predictable terrain from the world of child psychology.

Yet in her counter-memoir here, Jane casts doubt for the first time on her role in Jules's work.

What are readers to make of her narrative? What do Jane's accusations in *Choke Box* amount to? Truth? History? Recalibrated memory? An impossible, festering wound?

The current research of University of Massachusetts linguistics professor Alfred Knox Owen may shed light on, if not resolve, the controversy. His recent NEA grant—to algorithmically determine the probability of what he calls "parallel language production" in all Boward manuscripts (with the assistance of an FBI designed "data mining mechanism")— may be a determining factor in identifying their true authorship. His results, he warns, will not be conclusive, however.

Not only is "intra-familial language usage common," but his research suggests that "women, in particular, are encouraged from a young age to adopt the language of their male counterparts." His field calls this characteristic "ventrilingualism."

In short, Owen's conclusions will likely be of an uneven— what he calls, "dispositive"—nature. Though he expects he will be able to determine "whether" the same author wrote the books, and may even be able to determine "if" J.B. wrote his books himself, neither conclusion about J.B. is, in turn, proof-positive about Jane's authorship claim.

In short, even if Owen concludes that J.B. did *not* write his books, he cannot conclusively prove the obverse: that his sister Jane was their author instead.

Choke Box

Arguably an "epilogue" to J.B.'s nonfiction trilogy—*Living with Mother, Downward Dog,* and *What You Deserve*—Jane's *Choke Box* focuses on the author's adult life with her husband, Edward Tamlin (born Edvard Gyorgy Tzamlinskyia), and their children Robert Edward and Sophia Rose. Mother, Helena Boward, is a spectral presence in the text: influential, but absent. She appears in fewer than ten pages of the 143-page manuscript. Meanwhile, much as "Janey" was once absent from J.B.'s accounts, J.B. rarely appears in his sister's counter-memoir, though the reader is, for the first time, offered new details from the day of J.B.'s death that will no doubt satisfy his fan base. Until now, information about the teenager's death have been withheld from public consumption.

On its own merits, *Choke Box* can be read as the chronicle of one middle-aged woman's descent into madness. Evidence of a wealth of sociopathic conditions—some medical, others criminal—arises indiscriminately in its pages. For instance, Jane's claims that her husband, Edward Tamlin (who disappeared nine months before Jane Boward Tamlin's formal commitment at Buffalo Psychiatric Institute) was hiding out in their home, and that he could "control her like a character from a book with his words"[2] are clearly the insupportable accusations of a troubled mind. Moreover, the brief hospitalizations of her two children (for unrelated injuries) suggest that, late in her life, Jane became a threat to her children as much as to herself. Evidently, the courts agreed: against Jane's wishes, Helena Boward was granted guardianship of her grandchildren, Robert Edward and Sophia Rose.

Written in secret at Buffalo Psychiatric Institute, *Choke Box* was originally recovered by Jane Boward Tamlin's lawyer, Celeste Price, with the help of BPI's in-house therapist, Madeleine Hogue, and then sold to CounterSeed Press. Before the publisher could even confirm rumors about the forthcoming manuscript, however, Helena Boward stepped in with a restraining order. She has since claimed her legal maneuvers were designed only to validate what she has called

---

2. Edward Tamlin's book has disappeared much like its author. Meanwhile, documents show that, while Edward Tamlin did in fact request a leave from his position at the law offices of Hampton, Payne & Lynch LLC, it was for "undisclosed family reasons." The legal practice has refused to elaborate any further on this issue.

"the authorship, but not the authenticity of the manuscript." Though she lifted the restraining order after Price's and Hogue's arrests, and has allowed *Choke Box* to now be published, Helena Boward continues to refute all of Jane Boward Tamlin's claims in the book.

Choke Box: The Counter-Memoir

Critics agree that *Choke Box* sheds a fresh perspective on the scandal surrounding the Tamlins' demise. Certainly, it suggests that Jane did in fact suffer antinomy and deception of a unique order throughout her life—and that the full spectrum of her persecution, as she alleges throughout her counter-memoir, will in fact never be known. *Choke Box*, she tells us, was written for her children. However, its acute, often alarming, observations about motherhood—what she calls "the imperiled joy of raising children"—will touch a chord of uncomfortable familiarity in many parents.

"Nothing thicker than a knife's blade separates happiness from melancholy," Virginia Woolf reflects in *Orlando*. While Jane's narrative in *Choke Box* is colored by a similarly embittered joy, readers are counseled to keep an eye on the knife at the center of her memoir: whose hand holds it, conceals it, deploys it.

Alas, *Choke Box* often clouds the truth rather than clarifies.

As Jane might have said herself, "elusiveness" is a common trait in the Boward family gene pool.

Michel Saint-Trilit, PhD
Boward Chair of Media and Letters
University at Buffalo, SUNY

Text Credits

The following texts were sampled in the writing of this book:

Table, pages 66–67

"Once upon a time": Gertrude Stein, *Blood on the Dining Room Floor*

"Collaborators": Janet Kauffman, *Places in the World a Woman Could Walk*

"We go back": Marguerite Duras, *The Lover*

"I remember": Angela Carter, *The Bloody Chamber*

"She is here": Samantha Hunt, *The Invention of Everything Else*

"Reader, I married him": Charlotte Brontë, *Jane Eyre*

"It is commonly known": Mary Caponegro, *The Complexities of Intimacy*

"I closed the study door": Shirley Jackson, *Raising Demons*

"Could it be": Virginia Woolf, *Mrs. Dalloway*

"In a way": Toni Morrison, *Sula*

"What creature was it": Charlotte Brontë, *Jane Eyre*

"It was then": Joanna Scott, *Follow Me*

"Sometimes one meets a woman": Djuna Barnes, *Nightwood*

"You want to see": Marguerite Duras, *The Malady of Death*

"He had grabbed her": Nathalie Sarraute, *Tropisms*

"I am broken": H.D., *Hermione*

"The others relay": Theresa Hak Kyung Cha, *Dictee*

"I stood there": Kathy Acker, *Empire of the Senseless*

Table, pages 106–107

"What I am writing": Clarice Lispector, *Hour of the Star*

"So much has been taken": Rikki Ducornet, *The Fan-Maker's Inquisition*

"I am reminded": Christa Wolf, *Accident: A Day's News*

"If a physician": Charlotte Perkins Gilman, *The Yellow Wallpaper*

"I take another note": Lydia Davis, *The End of the Story*

"Shall we talk": Carole Maso, *Defiance*

"She takes my left arm": Theresa Hak Kyung Cha, *Dictee*

"She goes to the drawer": Janet Kauffman, *Places in the World a Woman Could Walk*

"The blood": Renee Gladman, *Newcomer Can't Swim*

"When your rage is choking you": Octavia E. Butler, *Fledgling*

"Qui vivra verra": Christine Brooke-Rose, *Amalgamemnon*

"I may be insane": Emily Holmes Coleman, *The Shutter of Snow*

"I am rising": Katherine Dunn, *Geek Love*

"Using the knife": Samantha Hunt, *The Invention of Everything Else*

"A person": Edie Meidav, *Kingdom of the Young*

"In other words": Shelley Jackson, *Half Life*

Acknowledgments

No book arrives in the world without literary accomplices, and it was my good fortune to be the recipient of the time and talents of several generous co-conspirators: Christine Hume, whose discerning eye and erudite observations are as vital to me as her friendship. Dave Kress, who offered encouragement and feedback with his distinctive, polymath enthusiasm. Ed Desautels, who bravely read this book in its most nascent stages. My parents and sister, who gave me the gift of their time when my time was thin. My daughters, Zazie and Xeni, whose irrepressible creative spirit has never failed to renew me. And Dimitri, who reads every word first and whose clarity remains an indispensable resource when the way feels dimly lighted.

To the community of women writers who have offered help, taken chances, led the way as editors, advisors, exemplars: thank you for your words on the page and in person. Without them, this book would not exist at all.

Many thanks to Ed Park and Brigid Hughes, who published a section of *Choke Box* in Akashic Books' *Buffalo Noir* as "Dr. Kirkbride's Moral Treatment Plan," and to the readers and editors of the Clarissa Dalloway Book Prize at the Room of Her Own Foundation and of the *Quarterly West* Novella Prize, who offered *Choke Box* crucial encouragement on their finalist lists. Finally, I'd like to thank the English Department at the University at Buffalo for supporting my work through a Dr. Nuala McGann Drescher Leave Award, which gave me much-needed time to launch this novel.

My very special thanks to Sabina Murray, who selected this book for the Juniper Prize, and to the exceptional team at the University of Massachusetts Press for giving me new cohorts and *Choke Box* a home.

JUNIPER

This volume is the seventeenth recipient
of the Juniper Prize for Fiction,
established in 2004 by the
University of Massachusetts Press
in collaboration with the
UMass Amherst MFA Program
for Poets and Writers, to be
presented annually for an outstanding
work of literary fiction. Like its sister award,
the Juniper Prize for Poetry established
in 1976, the prize is named in honor
of Robert Francis (1901–1987),
who lived for many years at
Fort Juniper, Amherst, Massachusetts.